TEMPLAR DETECTIVE

AND THE
UNHOLY EXORCIST

A TEMPLAR DETECTIVE THRILLER

Also by J. Robert Kennedy

James Acton Thrillers

The Protocol	*Blood Relics*
Brass Monkey	*Sins of the Titanic*
Broken Dove	*Saint Peter's Soldiers*
The Templar's Relic	*The Thirteenth Legion*
Flags of Sin	*Raging Sun*
The Arab Fall	*Wages of Sin*
The Circle of Eight	*Wrath of the Gods*
The Venice Code	*The Templar's Revenge*
Pompeii's Ghosts	*The Nazi's Engineer*
Amazon Burning	*Atlantis Lost*
The Riddle	*The Cylon Curse*

Special Agent Dylan Kane Thrillers

Rogue Operator	*Death to America*
Containment Failure	*Black Widow*
Cold Warriors	*The Agenda*
	Retribution

Delta Force Unleashed Thrillers

Payback	*The Lazarus Moment*
Infidels	*Kill Chain*
	Forgotten

Templar Detective Thrillers

The Templar Detective
The Templar Detective and the Parisian Adulteress
The Templar Detective and the Sergeant's Secret
The Templar Detective and the Unholy Exorcist

Detective Shakespeare Mysteries

Depraved Difference
Tick Tock
The Redeemer

Zander Varga, Vampire Detective

The Turned

THE TEMPLAR DETECTIVE

AND THE

UNHOLY EXORCIST

A TEMPLAR DETECTIVE THRILLER

J. ROBERT KENNEDY

ISBN-10: 172748746X

ISBN-13: 978-1727487466

First Edition

10 9 8 7 6 5 4 3 2 1

For my grandmother, Myrtle "Nanny" Lynk, stolen from us too soon.

THE TEMPLAR DETECTIVE

AND THE

UNHOLY EXORCIST

A TEMPLAR DETECTIVE THRILLER

"And there was in their synagogue a man with an unclean spirit; and he cried out, saying, Let us alone; what have we to do with thee, thou Jesus of Nazareth? Art thou come to destroy us? I know thee who thou art, the Holy One of God. And Jesus rebuked him, saying, Hold thy peace, and come out of him. And when the unclean spirit had torn him, and cried with a loud voice, he came out of him."

Mark 1:23-26, King James Version

"When the unclean spirit is gone out of a man, he walketh through dry places, seeking rest; and finding none, he saith, I will return unto my house whence I came out. And when he cometh, he findeth it swept and garnished. Then goeth he, and taketh to him seven other spirits more wicked than himself; and they enter in, and dwell there: and the last state of that man is worse than the first."

Luke 11:24-26, King James Version

AUTHOR'S NOTE

This is the fourth novel in this series, and for those who have read the others and embraced these characters as so many of you have, please feel free to skip this note, as you will have already read it.

The word "detective" is believed to have originated in the mid-nineteenth century, however, that doesn't mean the concept of someone who investigated crime originated less than two hundred years ago. Crime long pre-dated this era, and those who investigated it as well.

The following historical thriller is intended to be an entertaining read for all, with the concept of a "Templar Detective" a fun play on a modern term. The dialog is intentionally written in such a way that today's audiences can relate, as opposed to how people might have spoken in Medieval France, where, of course, they would have conversed in French and not English, with therefore completely different manners of speaking. This does not mean they will be speaking to each other as rappers and gangsters, but will instead communicate in ways that imply comfort and familiarity, as we would today. If you are expecting, "Thou dost hath offended me, my good sir," then prepareth thyself for disappointment. If, however, you are looking for a fast-paced adventure, with plenty of action, mystery, and humor, then you've come to the right place.

Enjoy.

PREFACE

The concept of demonic possession is featured prominently in the Bible and other holy texts, as well as the oral histories of many cultures. Saving these lost souls was the duty of shamans, medicine men or women, and eventually, in Catholicism, priests.

And the task was never taken lightly. While there were few rules initially against undertaking the task, as the Bible indicated even laypeople could perform exorcisms in the name of Jesus Christ, by the Middle Ages, it was mostly the work of priests, and laypeople were forbidden from using any of the prayers reserved for priests when performing an exorcism.

Today, most believe that those possessed by demons are actually mentally ill, often schizophrenics, and their "demonic" symptoms are merely those of their affliction. This understanding, however, is relatively new, and few, if any, in medieval France, would have even considered mental illness as a possibility, leaving thousands to be treated as evil, requiring the services of an exorcist to save them from damnation.

These well-meaning clergymen were performing these rituals at what they felt was great risk to themselves, to save those who didn't need saving, where a lack of scientific understanding, that void filled with superstition, led to the torture of thousands.

But what if the tables were turned?

Outside Crécy-la-Chapelle, Kingdom of France

1298 AD

Isabelle Leblanc hugged her knees tight, long having given up tugging at the irons gripping her ankles, the chains binding her to the others suffering the same fate. Whimpering, crying women, all young like her, pleading to be let go, begging to be returned to their homes, or some, like her, sitting in numbed silence, trying to make sense of what had happened.

They were held in a type of wagon she had never seen, one with metal bars for sides. It was freezing cold, the elements of a blustery January provided no challenge by the gaps in the bars, nor by their clothes, as they had been taken from their homes as they had been found, with no time given to change.

She herself had been torn from her home, dragged to the village center, and accused of the most heinous of things by a priest she had never seen before, supported by twelve monks in long dark robes, none of whom had revealed their faces. These men, now on horseback, surrounded the wagon driven by the priest she had heard referred to as Father Mercier, providing protection to the small procession as it moved, she presumed, to the next town to kidnap yet another victim.

Yet that wasn't what was going on at all, if Mercier was to be believed.

If the priest was to be taken at his word, they were all possessed by demons, and he was taking them to save their souls, to rid them of the evil that possessed them, and when finished, they would be returned home to their families, cleansed of that which had taken them over.

But she wasn't possessed.

She couldn't be.

Could she?

Would she even know?

She assumed she would, though perhaps that was part of the trickery of the Devil at play. And these other women with her? With the exception of the creature in the far corner, none seemed anything but normal. Though the exception was anything but. A snarling, barking mess of a woman, barely recognizable as human, clearly possessed by something not of this earth.

And she terrified them all.

She alone lent credence to this entire situation.

A situation she had no idea how she would escape.

If only Sir Marcus were here!

Sir Marcus de Rancourt, a Templar Knight who now lived in her village with his sergeant and two squires, had left for business in Paris

6

earlier this very day. If he had been there, he would have come for her, she was certain.

Shouts behind them snapped her from her spiral of self-pity, and had her pressed against the bars along with the others, as three horses galloped past then blocked the path of the wagon. An angry conversation was taking place, only the stray word caught, but it didn't matter.

She knew these men.

And they were here for her.

David and Jeremy, the two squires of Sir Marcus.

And the bastard Garnier, responsible for her current situation.

She had been saved.

Relief washed over her and her shoulders heaved as tears of joy erupted.

Then she froze.

The monks surrounding the wagon tossed their robes aside and drew swords, pointing them toward the new arrivals.

This can't be happening!

It made no sense. Armed monks?

Then the wagon moved again.

What's going on?

She pressed against the bars, shoving her head through as they passed David, Jeremy, and Garnier. She stretched out a hand toward them, and she saw David stop Jeremy from taking it.

"Please! Help me!"

David's head sank in shame, and Jeremy stared at her, tears in his eyes, as Garnier covered his face.

"Why have you forsaken me?" she cried, stretching through the bars even farther, but she was given no answer, only helpless stares filled with regret.

She collapsed back to the floor, her arm still shoved through the bars, her sobs racking her body in waves. Why had they let them take her? Why had these men, whom she considered friends, allowed her to be kidnapped by this priest, who claimed she was possessed? Didn't they know she wasn't? Didn't they know she was innocent? Didn't they know Father Mercier had made a mistake?

She curled into a ball, praying to God for forgiveness for whatever it was she had done that was so horrible, it deserved a punishment such as this.

And as she prayed for deliverance from this exorcist who had taken her, her thoughts turned to the sin she had committed that day against poor Garnier, and she knew, deep down, exactly why she was here, condemned with the others.

And part of her felt she deserved whatever punishment the Lord had in store for her.

Chantilly Forest, Kingdom of France
One week earlier

Father Mercier flicked the reins, his heart at once filled with the power of the Lord, and the ache of the pain he shared with those locked away behind him, their poor souls awaiting the deliverance he would soon bring them. While it was the demons that possessed them that wailed and cried in protest, begging their demonic lord to free them from their shackles, those innocent souls trapped within would have their possessors exorcised in due course.

It wouldn't be long before the wagon was full, then they would return to his church, perform the rituals, and if successful, return the innocent left behind to their families and loved ones. He smiled, drawing a deep breath, as he thought of all the good he had done over the past couple of years.

"You seem happy."

Father Mercier nodded. "I am. Doing the Lord's work always makes me happy."

"There is no better work."

"I agree. And though it shames me to think of a reward for all I have done, I still take solace in what you told me."

"Of your mother?"

"Yes." He stole a quick glance at his companion. "Of how you said her condemned soul would be freed by what we are doing here."

"And it will be, I assure you. You simply have to have faith."

Mercier's chest ached with the words. "You know my faith never wavers."

"As it shouldn't. The work you do is necessary, and may take a lifetime, but the countless souls you are saving through your sacrifice will not only grant you access into the Kingdom of Heaven, but your mother as well."

Mercier's smile spread. "That's all I want. My own fate is not why I do this. It is all for my mother, and for the poor wretched souls like those young women behind me."

"You are a good man."

A rush of pride washed through him. "From you, that means everything." He stared past the escort in front of him, noticing another carriage approaching on the narrow road. He pulled the wagon as far to the side as he could, his escort of one dozen devout monks, specially trained to deal with the demons he encountered on an almost daily basis, guiding their horses out of the way as well.

The carriage approached slowly on the snow-covered road, the coachman and his companion both tipping their hats as they passed.

Mercier bowed his head with a smile, then as the carriage came up beside him, he saw a beautiful creature lean out the window, her long blond hair in curls, topped with the prettiest of hats, her cheeks a rosy glow brought on by the chill in the air, and some sort of applied reddish hue.

She was clearly from a wealthy family, and her manner of dress and bearing suggested a pampered upbringing, unlike those behind him. Her beauty suggested she had been sculpted by the most gifted of artisans.

And such beauty, he knew, would never have been created by God's hand, for no woman should ever be so beautiful. This was the work of the most evil of all artisans.

This was the work of Satan himself.

He stared at her, a smile of recognition at what he had stumbled upon spreading. And she returned the smile, a smile that soon turned into a sneer, her eyes glaring back at him, red, wicked, as if the flames of Hell burned behind them.

He had found another lost soul, another example of the Devil's work.

He held up a hand, and the demon's coachman brought her carriage to a halt. She leaned farther out the window, hurling insults at him, sputtering and cursing in the language known only to the possessed, but Mercier ignored it, for he had heard it all before, and he would hear it again, probably before the day was through.

He reached under his vestments and withdrew the wooden cross given to him by his mother years ago, before she had been lost to him. She too had been an uncommonly beautiful woman, though his memories of her were fading with time, as he was young when she had been taken. Like those behind him, like the creature in front of him, his mother had been possessed by evil, as so many young beautiful women were, the voices she claimed were in her head telling her to do unspeakable things.

His father had been forced to take action, to take her to the local priest, yet despite his best efforts to rid her of the evil that possessed her, she had succumbed, her soul in the end saved through her passing, though condemned in Purgatory for the sins the flesh had committed.

He had stood in the corner, sobbing unnoticed as the demon possessing his mother had fought the incantations, fought the holy water, fought the symbols of the Church, all the while writhing and snarling against those who would restrain her. It was something he now knew no child should have witnessed, yet he had, and there was no unseeing the evil present that day.

And it had changed him.

He had decided his future lay in the priesthood, so he could save the souls of these poor, cursed women, so no other child would suffer the loss he had. Through the good Lord, he would use His divine power to rid these women, condemned from the moment of birth with their beauty, beauty that could be used to tempt good men into unholy acts.

For it was their beauty, sculpted by Satan himself, that the demons possessing them would use to their own ends to threaten God's dominion over man, to further the foothold of evil that one day might overwhelm the forces of good.

He had vowed that day, the day his mother had died, to save every woman he could. And here, today, he had found yet another.

His constant companion confirmed what he already knew. "She's one of them. We must save her."

"I know. But she has a guard. They won't believe me."

"They often don't, yet you always succeed."

Mercier sighed, smiling sadly at the coachman and his companion. He didn't blame them. They weren't at fault. It was rare that those living with the possessed could recognize the evil in their souls. While he saw the snarling beasts for what they were, those around them only saw the beauty.

It led the innocent to do the bidding of the evil in their midst.

The demon's chaperone appeared in the window, a plain woman, clearly not afflicted as her charge was. "What is the meaning of this?"

"I am Father Mercier. I must ask your mistress to come with me."

The escort expressed surprise, but the demon merely stared at him, her glowing eyes and her curled mouth in constant motion as it assessed the situation.

He returned the stare, the pity he felt written on his face for the lost soul beneath the hate, pity the demon was having nothing of, more of Satan's vile tongue erupting from her. He sighed, reciting a brief prayer for strength. "I'm sorry, my child, but your suffering will soon be over."

He raised a hand then dropped it, signaling his escort to take her. And as the monks surged forward, their swords drawn, he closed his eyes and prayed for the souls of those who would be slain here today. For their deaths would not be in vain. This child would be saved, her soul cleansed, and she would be returned to her family the pure vessel God had always meant her to be.

De Rancourt Residence
Crécy-la-Chapelle, Kingdom of France
One week later

Isabelle Leblanc wasn't sure why she felt so comfortable with Lady Joanne de Rohan. Perhaps it was that the woman treated her as an equal, though in an often paternalistic way, the age gap significant. But Isabelle didn't mind. The woman was very wise, far better educated than anyone she had ever met, and had such interesting stories about life in Paris as part of the ruling class.

Of course, that was all over for the poor woman now. She had lost everything in a scandal that had rocked the King's Court, and now lived on the farm owned by Sir Marcus de Rancourt, a farm that was quickly becoming a safe haven for wayward souls. The Templar Knight had inherited the farm when his sister had died last year, and he had reluctantly agreed to remain and raise her orphaned son and daughter rather than return to the Holy Land. His loyal sergeant, Simon Chastain, and his squires, David and Jeremy, had also pledged to remain with their master and friend.

And in less than a year, another orphaned boy now lived here, along with Lady Joanne and her chambermaid, Beatrice.

It was a lively farm now, and a place she felt comfortable. When Marcus' sister, Nicoline, had passed, preceded several years before by her husband, Sir Henri de Foix, a nearly destitute man with royal lineage, Isabelle and her mother had taken care of the farm and the children until Sir Marcus could return. She had been happy to do it, for she had grand expectations for his arrival.

She intended to marry him.

She had been in love with him for years, though she had never met him. All she knew were the stories Nicoline had shared with her about her gallant brother, the Templar Knight, a man his own sister hadn't seen in two decades. And when he had arrived, he was everything she had imagined and more. Incredibly handsome, strong, brave.

And celibate.

He and his men had been granted special dispensation to remain members of the Order, the Poor Fellow-Soldiers of Christ and of the Temple of Solomon, so long as they maintained their vows.

He had never expressed any interest in her, and it had frustrated her to no end. It had meant that she'd have to find someone to marry other than the man that had merely been a young girl's fantasy.

Then Thomas Durant had arrived.

And she had fallen madly in love.

"Where are you, child?"

Isabelle flinched then looked at Lady Joanne. "Excuse me?"

"Where are you? You're definitely not here."

Isabelle flushed. "Sorry, I was thinking of something."

Beatrice snickered as her needle and thread rapidly worked its magic on a torn shirt belonging to one of the children. "Young Thomas, I bet!"

Isabelle's cheeks burned.

Joanne smiled at her from behind her cup of hot tisane. "You two have been exchanging quite a few letters."

Now her ears were afire.

"Your reading and writing have improved dramatically since I've been here."

Beatrice snorted. "Nothing like the love of a good man to make one try new things."

"Beatrice!" cried Joanne, smacking her chambermaid's shoulder. "The children are in the next room."

Beatrice shrugged. "Nothing they won't hear soon enough."

Joanne shook her head. "You're incorrigible."

"Which I believe is why you keep me around."

Joanne patted her companion, once her servant, now her equal. "You do keep me sane." She turned to Isabelle. "I suppose your mother has been pressuring you to find a husband, now that this nonsense with Sir Marcus is finished with?"

Isabelle flushed even more, if that were possible. How could the woman possibly have known about her irrational obsession with the man? "How—"

"How did I know?" Joanne regarded her with a look of pity. "My

16

poor girl, everyone knows."

She gulped. "And Sir Marcus? Does he know?"

"With the amount of teasing he gets from his men, I'd say so."

Isabelle's shoulders slumped. "I'm so embarrassed."

Joanne leaned over and gave her forearm a squeeze. "Think nothing of it, young one. All young girls have crushes, it's part of being a girl. Why, you wouldn't believe some of the boys—and men—I had feelings for, certain I would be marrying them as soon as I was of age. Instead, I ended up marrying—"

"A bastard."

Joanne chuckled at Beatrice. "Yes, in the end. But we did have some good days before he did what he did." She returned her attention to Isabelle. "So, Thomas Durant. Does your mother approve?"

Isabelle snorted. "Not at all! Mother wants me to have nothing to do with him."

"Whatever for?"

"She's heard about his vocation, and his father's."

Joanne frowned. "That's unfortunate, though a boy should never be blamed for the sins of his father."

"That's what I tried to tell her, but once she found out who he's now working for, she won't listen." Isabelle sighed. "And I understand. I hate what Thomas does."

Joanne put down her empty cup, Beatrice refilling it before her former mistress could, a servant's old habits hard to break. "It is unfortunate that he's working for such a horrid woman, but he had little choice. He was starving to death, from what I heard. If it weren't for that job, he wouldn't have survived the winter."

"He could have come here. Sir Marcus did offer him the choice."

17

"Abandoning one's home is difficult." Joanne frowned. "Trust me, if anyone knows, I do." She forced a smile. "He'll come around. In time, he'll want to marry you, and make a life here with you."

"Not if my mother has anything to say about it. Can you believe she wants me to marry Garnier?"

Beatrice roared with laughter. "Garnier? That awkward one who lives on the other side of the village?"

Isabelle nodded. "Yes!"

Beatrice placed her work in her lap rather than risk puncturing herself as she continued to laugh. "Oh, he's a *fine* one, that one is."

Isabelle felt a little guilty. "He's nice. I mean, he's always been nice to me."

"Of course he is, lass, have you seen yourself? You're the prettiest thing in this village." Beatrice leaned forward. "There's not a man or boy within a day's ride who wouldn't give his right hand to be with you."

Isabelle blushed again. "I'm sure I don't know what you mean."

Beatrice elbowed Joanne. "I'm sure she does!"

Joanne shook her head at her chambermaid with a frown. "You're terrible. Things aren't like the city, here." She turned to Isabelle. "Ignore her. I'm sure Garnier is a fine young man."

"He is."

"But he's no Thomas, am I right?"

Isabelle shrugged.

"Tell me why you like him so much."

Isabelle smiled as a warmth spread through her entire body, a tingling emerging that threatened to become embarrassingly personal.

18

"He excites me like no one else ever has."

"Even our handsome Templar Knight?" asked Beatrice with a wink.

"Yes, even him." She sighed. "You're right, that was a foolish girl's fantasy, fed by his sister's constant talking of how great a man he was, when she didn't even really know him."

Joanne wagged a finger. "A sister knows her brother."

"Not when she hasn't seen him in over twenty years, and rarely wrote her back."

"That may be, but was she so wrong in her impression of him?"

Isabelle frowned. "No, I suppose not. He *is* brave and caring, and truly a good man."

Beatrice cleared her throat. "Not to mention the fact he fills out a pair of pants quite nicely."

"Beatrice!" cried Joanne before bursting into laughter. "You really are terrible!"

Isabelle tried to stifle her own laughter. "He *is* handsome, there's no doubt of that, and he would make a fine husband and provider for any children we might be blessed with, but he has made his feelings clear. He intends to maintain his vows."

Beatrice grunted. "Celibacy! What a boring way to live!"

More laughter erupted from the older ladies.

Joanne stopped first. "The life of a Templar Knight is a simple one. Nothing to excess, and so much denied. All in exchange to serve your Lord, and gain entry into the Kingdom of Heaven."

Beatrice picked up her needle once again. "A worthy goal. But to deny oneself all the wonders that the good Lord above has provided for his flock?"

Joanne shrugged. "Some would say that these wonders are the work of the Devil, and that the Templars will be rewarded for recognizing that."

Isabelle stared at the older woman, a woman she respected tremendously. "Do you really think that things like love, and the joys of marriage, are things that the Lord would deny us?"

"If that were true, why'd he make them feel so good?" cackled Beatrice, Joanne smiling.

"Child, you're still young. Find yourself the right man, marry him, bear him a bunch of children and raise them right, and you'll be just as welcome in Heaven as any Templar, I assure you."

Isabelle nodded slowly, then shrugged. "I've never really concerned myself with such things. I go to church, try to obey the Commandments as best I can, and live a good life. What more could the Lord ask?"

Joanne smiled. "Absolutely nothing."

Beatrice agreed, then added her usual slant. "But why shouldn't that good life be with a looker, hey? If not Sir Marcus, then your young Thomas I think will fit the bill. He's got a tasty little narrow ass on him!" She roared with laughter, Joanne turning red before joining in, as Isabelle blushed then giggled.

Joanne regained control first. "Whomever you choose, just don't settle for someone you don't love. I made that mistake, and look what it cost me. My husband has been executed, I've lost my family, my title, and now here I live as humbly as my once servant"—she patted Beatrice on the knee—"because I chose poorly."

Isabelle's heart ached for the woman. "Is it really that bad? I mean, life here, living like we do?"

Joanne sighed. "To be honest, at first, yes. But now, after so many months have passed, I find I'm quite content in this new life."

"Would you prefer the old?"

Joanne frowned. "Some days I think yes, but most, no. My responsibilities here are much simpler. Keep the men fed and in clean clothes and bedding, keep them washed every once in a while"—Isabelle snickered—"and tend to those beautiful children. I no longer have to worry about impressing the high society of Paris, deal with their snobbery, or bother with the Court and the miscreants it attracts. Here, everyone is equal, with the same problems, and the same responsibilities." She glanced about the humble home. "And I dare say we have it better than most. With four healthy, strong men to do much of the work, and a small legacy left by my cousin to provide a slightly finer home"—Isabelle glanced at the actual glass in the windows with some envy—"life here is fairly comfortable." Joanne smiled at the others. "And I have such good friends here that I can talk to frankly and honestly. *That* is something I never truly had back in Paris." She smiled at Isabelle. "You must marry the man you love, the man who will be your partner and confidante in this hard life. Only then will you truly be happy."

Isabelle frowned. Everything said was true, and in a perfect world, she'd follow the advice without hesitation. But there was one roadblock. "But what of Mother? She still insists I marry Garnier!"

"Have Thomas prove to her that he loves you, and that he can provide for you, and in time, she'll come to realize that, and give him her blessing."

"I fear she won't, at least not until he changes his line of work."

Beatrice grunted. "You shouldn't have told her that."

Isabelle's eyes shot wide. "I had to! She's my mother!"

"Mothers shouldn't know all the secrets their daughters possess."

Joanne apparently agreed. "You must make it clear to your mother that this Garnier boy is *not* in your future, so that she can stop pestering you with it, and stop leading the poor boy on."

Isabelle sighed. "If only he weren't so awkward, I would probably have been happy marrying him. But he's just so embarrassing to be around."

A sound at the window had them all leaping to their feet, Tanya, their large mastiff, curled up by the fire, rushing for the door. Isabelle grabbed her by the scruff of the neck as she opened it. Her heart sank as she gasped at the sight of poor Garnier running away, the boy glancing back over his shoulder, his eyes red, his cheeks stained with tears.

He had heard everything they had said about him.

"Garnier! Please come back!"

But he didn't, instead leaning into his escape from their horrid barbs at his expense. She traced his footsteps in the snow back to the window to the left side of the house, and her shoulders slumped. A bundle of dried flowers lay on the ground, flowers she found on her doorstep at home every week, fresh when in season, and lovingly preserved when not.

"What have I done?" she sobbed as she stared after the poor boy.

"*You've* done nothing, my dear," said Joanne, now at her side. "But I'm afraid I have. I never should have said such things about him, or let such things be said."

Isabelle shook her head. "You couldn't have known he was

listening."

Joanne put an arm over her shoulders. "It doesn't matter. Things like that should never be said, even when believed to be out of earshot."

"What am I going to do?"

"I fear there's nothing much you can do. His heart is broken, and only time or a new love can heal it. Let us hope, however, that this puts an end to his interest in you, so everyone can move on."

"I should talk to him."

"Absolutely not! It will only hurt him more, because he now knows how you feel. Let him heal in his own way, then when the time is right, you'll encounter him again, you'll tell him you miss his friendship, and that you hope things can go back to the way they were when you were young. Perhaps that will allow you both to move on and save him from the embarrassment he now feels."

Isabelle stared up the hill toward the barracks, a wisp of smoke lazily rising into the still air, the four Templars that protected them inside, laughter rolling down the snow-covered fields.

She sighed.

Things would have been so much easier if Sir Marcus had fulfilled the desires of the little girl who had grown up to love him so deeply.

But life never turns out the way one hopes.

De Rancourt Residence
Crécy-la-Chapelle, Kingdom of France

"Is that young Garnier?"

Templar Knight Sir Marcus de Rancourt glanced out the door of their barracks and down the hill, spotting only the back of whoever had been at the home. "Looks like it."

His sergeant, Simon Chastain, shook his head. "I've never seen him run so fast without tripping."

Jeremy, one of Marcus' trusted squires, and a master with the bow, snorted. "That one's so awkward, he wouldn't have lasted a week in the Crusades."

David, Marcus' other squire and the older of the two, stretched. "I'd have given him a day."

"I was trying to be generous."

"Generosity only gets people killed over there."

Marcus nodded. "I didn't realize the ladies had guests, the way they were carrying on."

Simon grunted. "Women. I'll never understand them."

David grinned. "Because they'll never let you close enough."

Simon jabbed a finger at him. "We all are bound by the same vows, so don't you be suggesting otherwise."

David flushed slightly at the admonishment. "You're right, you're right. Sometimes I forget we're still part of the Order."

Marcus regarded the man for a moment. They were all still technically members of the Order, all still Templars, though their lives with their brothers were essentially over. Unless some calamity was to occur, to which they were dutybound to respond, the rest of their days would be spent mostly on this farm. It was a decision he had been forced to make, with only one honorable choice, but the others had stayed of their own free will. "You can disavow yourself of the Order if you want."

"I thought we already had this discussion?" David shook his head. "My place is at your side, and I do it willingly."

Marcus smiled slightly. "No, that's not what I meant. You could leave the Order and stay here, at my side as you say, but be free to take a wife and start a family."

David scratched his chin. "I hadn't thought of that."

Jeremy leaned back. "That's because you're an idiot."

David belted his friend's shoulder, then leaned back as well. "I'm too old to start a family, aren't I?"

Marcus shrugged. "You're asking the wrong person." He turned to Simon. "Sergeant?"

Simon gave him a look. "Are you mad? I know less of these things than you!"

They all laughed, the children suddenly appearing in the door. "What's so funny?" asked Pierre Fabron, an orphaned boy they had taken in after his parents had been murdered.

Marcus searched for an appropriate answer. "Ahh, nothing you'd understand."

"Nor apparently us," muttered David.

Jeremy pointed toward the stable. "So, have the horses been fed?"

"Yes, sir," replied Pierre.

"Good." Jeremy stood, David following. "We'll finish readying your horses."

Marcus nodded, and his two squires left to prepare the horses for his and Simon's trip to Paris, a day's ride to the west. He sighed.

"What?"

He glanced at his sergeant and friend of over twenty years. "They should leave the Order and take wives. It's not too late for them."

Simon grunted. "But it is for us?"

"Certainly for me."

Simon regarded him. "The way that young Isabelle was fawning over you for so long, I think you could have your pick."

"I have no idea why."

"I think it's your chiseled good looks and fine piece of ass you keep hidden under that surcoat."

Marcus laughed, shaking his head. "I'm far too old for such a young thing, and besides, I'm too set in my ways. Look at me. This is now my farm, yet I live in the barracks with you."

"Only because Lady Joanne now occupies your bedchamber." Simon's eyebrows shot up. "Now there's an idea. She's a widow. You two could get married."

Marcus rolled his eyes. "Right, a former member of the aristocracy marrying a former Templar Knight. If that's not a recipe for disaster, I don't know what is."

Simon grunted. "True. I think we'll have to resign ourselves to remaining in the Order, celibate, with only each other for company."

Marcus groaned. "Well, when you put it that way, it doesn't sound like much of a life."

Simon stared at him. "I think I've just been insulted."

"You have."

"Perhaps when we go to Paris for this meeting of yours, I should find myself a new master."

"You could try, though I think you'll have a hard time finding one who's willing to put up with your attitude."

"I've got a great attitude."

"You're a crusty old bastard that takes a long time to get used to."

"You got used to me."

Marcus' eyes narrowed. "My friend, it's been twenty years and I'm just about there." He pointed to the heavens. "I'm not sure God is willing to leave you down here long enough for anyone new to get used to you."

Simon shook his head. "You're not the easiest to get along with either, you know."

Marcus grinned. "You *will* find me delightful, Sergeant, that's an order."

Simon laughed. "Yes, m'Lord, you are definitely a delight."

Marcus' stomach rumbled, Simon hearing it. "I think we should see what the ladies have prepared us for breakfast. I want to get on the road soon so we aren't late arriving in Paris. This weather can be unpredictable."

"My bones tell me we're due for a storm soon."

Marcus pushed to his feet with a groan. "Mine as well, old man." They began for the house at the bottom of the gentle hill, the laughter of the women having stopped since Garnier had been spotted running away. It was unfortunate that he was sweet on Isabelle, as her heart was now taken by Thomas Durant, a young man Marcus intended to visit later that evening after his meeting at the Enclos du Temple, the Templar headquarters in the Kingdom of France.

He opened the door with a smile, then frowned at what greeted him.

Two unhappy women.

And one *very* unhappy woman.

"What happened?"

And he immediately regretted asking the question.

Crécy-la-Chapelle, Kingdom of France

Garnier's heart hammered in horror at the scene unfolding in front of him. He had suffered nightmares before, but not even his deepest darkest imaginings could rival what was happening now. A wagon with iron bars sat in the middle of their village, a dozen monks, all dressed in dark brown robes, encircled the terror, their hoods covering their features, leaving their faces blackened orbs as if part of the evil they now guarded his fellow villagers from. Each held a torch, the only light except for the large fire roaring in the middle of the road, all casting an eerie, flickering glow upon the priest that had arrived as the last hint of the winter sun set, leaving the small, simple village in a cloak of darkness.

The timing of their arrival had been perfect, the priest calling for everyone to gather for an important message from the Church, and Garnier had been fetched from his home by a neighbor, arriving only minutes before as the creature now before them had been led from her cage, a growling, snarling, spitting, filthy thing, screaming vile profanities at those surrounding her.

If ever there was a demon in their midst, it was today.

"No! Don't look away! Look at her in all her vileness," said the priest, his voice calm but earnest. "Look at what Satan himself has done to this poor creature. Remember, the soul trapped within is innocent of anything her body does, anything her lips say. She is locked away inside, a prisoner in her own body. Remember, she is someone's daughter, someone's sister, and yes, could be someone's mother. Pity her, but don't fear her, not in this state. She has been captured, and with prayer, I intend to save her soul, as I intend to save all those possessed in our troubled land. Now, I ask of you, have you any like her among you?"

Garnier shook his head slowly, as did the others of the village, then cried out in horror as the creature flipped over, her back arched, her hands and feet still flat on the ground as she walked as if turned inside out, something he had never seen anything, man or beast, ever do.

He collapsed to a knee, reaching out to steady himself as others fainted around him in terror, some turning to vomit, prayer erupting from those who still remained in control of their faculties.

"Good! Pray! Pray to our good Lord for salvation, for delivery from evil such as this! Pray for the soul of this poor woman, and keep her in your prayers, for only through the power of prayer will she be saved! Now, I ask you again, are there any like her among you?"

Garnier pushed to his feet, wiping his forehead of the sweat that now beaded on it, and again shook his head.

"Then you are fortunate, for this one is so far gone, she will be difficult to save. But hear this! Most are not so far gone as her. Even she wasn't this far gone when I first captured her. But resigned to its fate, the demon inside her is now desperate, and knows it has been discovered. It no longer has any need to hide its true nature. Among you, among those of you gathered here tonight, there may yet be one of the possessed. Or perhaps they ignored my call, and are still in their homes, hiding from me, because they know that I alone possess the ability to see their true nature, to see through the masks they show their neighbors. What you see as a normal neighbor, the man or woman you have perhaps grown up with, beneath could be a beast like this. So again, I ask you, is there someone who is not here tonight, who ignored my call for a message from the Church, someone who may be a demon among you?"

Garnier looked about in the darkness, the faces of the people he had grown up with his entire young life surrounding the spectacle, and frowned. Easily half the village wasn't here. Almost none of the children were, and most of the women weren't as well, probably at home with the children preparing dinner. It was the men who were here, who would carry back any message to their families, as would he. His family remained at home, even his father, sending Garnier to hear what the priest had to say, then share it when he came home.

"Still, you can think of no one? Then let me share another secret Satan doesn't want you to know. Did you know that beauty is the work of the Devil? Why would God ever create a woman so beautiful she would make a man do foolish things? Why would He create someone so breathtaking that men would fight over her, that jealousies would flare? No, God would never do such a thing, but Satan would." The priest continued to circle the fire, leading the wretched creature, still twisted in an unnatural state that Garnier couldn't bring himself to look at. "Is there anyone among you who is so beautiful, she has caused the men around her to do foolish things?"

"Isabelle!"

He slapped both of his hands over his mouth, shocked and sickened that he had blurted out her name. His eyes widened as everyone turned toward him, the priest rushing forward.

"What was that you said?"

Garnier was shaking now, trying to figure out why he had shouted out the name of the woman he had loved until only hours before, before she had destroyed all the love he had, all the plans for their future together, and any confidence he might have had.

Her beauty was unparalleled in this small village, he had done foolish things to win her heart, and she had emasculated him with no regard for his feelings.

It was the cold-heartedness of what had been said that made him realize that no good Christian could be living at that farm. And it had all changed when those Templars arrived.

The priest shook him by the shoulder. "Young man, who did you name?"

"I, umm…" He stared at the ground. "May I ask a question?"

"Of course, my son, of course. What is your question?"

"Could a demon have been brought back from the Holy Land, and then moved into the body of someone here?"

The priest nodded vigorously. "Of course! There is much evil in the Holy Land. For one of Satan's minions to come here to spread his terrible ways to our kingdom is definitely possible." The priest stepped closer, his face only inches from Garnier's. "Why? Do you think this has happened to someone you know?" He leaned even closer. "Someone you love?"

Garnier sucked in a deep breath. "She's changed. Since those Templars arrived, she hasn't been the same. Maybe they returned from the Holy Land with some sort of evil."

"What is her name, my son?"

"Isabelle. Isabelle Leblanc."

"And is she beautiful?"

"Yes, absolutely!"

"Uncommonly beautiful?"

"I should say she's the most beautiful girl in the village."

The priest spun toward the others, congregating around Garnier. "And would you agree, my good people? Would you agree that Isabelle Leblanc is beautiful?"

Nods of assent were reluctantly given.

"Uncommonly so?"

The nods grew in confidence.

He turned back to Garnier. "Is she married?"

Garnier shook his head.

"So, she is yet a virgin?"

Garnier gulped, uncomfortable with the question. "I-I would expect so."

The priest smiled. "She is exactly what the Devil seeks. The purest of vessels that he can corrupt with beauty that could tempt any man." He turned to the crowd. "And would you say she's changed since these Templars arrived?"

"I should say so!" shouted someone from the back. "She's been making a fool of herself chasing that Templar Knight!"

The priest smiled, then turned back to Garnier. "So, we have an uncommonly beautiful woman who has changed her behavior since a group of Templars have returned from the Holy Land." He threw his hands in the air as he quickly stepped back toward the fire. "I say to you, my good people, that Isabelle Leblanc is the reason the good Lord brought me here this night. The good Lord told me I would find evil in this village, and He was right. Give me this girl, and I will save her soul, and return her to you, return the loving, caring girl you all once knew, cleansed of the evil brought back from the Holy Land by these Templars."

Garnier hesitated, his stomach churning as he doubted his own twisted thoughts of only moments ago, now that the demand for Isabelle to be brought forward had been made. "But how will you know? How will you know she is possessed?"

The priest shook his chain, the creature at the other end growling then flipping upright. "The possessed know each other. Give her to me, and we will see how this one reacts to her."

"I'll go get her!" shouted someone.

"And I!"

The priest waved a hand, halting the men already heading for Isabelle's home. "No. These demons can be dangerous when confronted. My monks have been trained for these very situations." He pointed at Garnier. "Show them where she lives, and my men will take care of the rest."

Garnier nodded reluctantly, and led them toward the small house near the edge of the village, a house he had visited hundreds, perhaps thousands of times in his life, his friendship with Isabelle stretching back to before he could remember.

And now here, today, he had betrayed her, all because of the hurt he felt inside.

His mouth filled with bile as he stretched out a hand, pointing toward the home where the love of his life lived. A love he had just forsaken, for he knew in his heart she was innocent, and that everything she had said, though painful, was true.

He was awkward.

He was embarrassing.

And he didn't deserve to be loved.

He collapsed to his knees, his shoulders racked with sobs as the monks pressed forward.

Lord, what have I done?

Leblanc Residence

Crécy-la-Chapelle, Kingdom of France

"I feel just terrible."

Isabelle's mother frowned at her. "As you should. It was horrible what you said. And those women should know better than to talk like that." She wagged a finger. "I don't think I want you spending any more time over there. I think they're a bad influence, especially that Beatrice. She seems most uncouth."

Isabelle's jaw dropped. "But, Mother, they're my friends!"

"They're too old to be your friends."

"It's not like there's a lot of people my age here. At least not to talk to."

"That's because they all have husbands to talk to. You wasted too much time spurning anyone who tried to court you for too long. If I had known why, that it was Nicoline filling your head with stories about her brother, and that you had gone and fallen in love with a man who would never have you, I would have slapped some sense into you long ago."

Isabelle sat in silence, her chin on her chest, her hands folded in her lap, as the tirade she had heard so many times before repeated itself. The sad thing was her mother was right. Almost every boy in the village had called on her, and she had turned them all away. Only poor Garnier hadn't given up, but that was merely because he had no prospects.

"Are you even listening to me?"

"Is there any point?"

Her mother raised her hand and Isabelle recoiled. "You talk to your daughter. I'm not getting through."

Her father, sitting by the fire warming his feet, grunted. "Leave the poor girl alone. She has a suitor. One with means, apparently."

Her mother threw up her hands. "Don't get me started on that Thomas character. Do you really want your daughter marrying a criminal?"

"If it will shut you up, I'd let her marry the bloody horse."

Isabelle snickered, but a glare from her mother put an end to it.

"Tomorrow, you will go to Garnier and apologize. The poor boy doesn't deserve what you did."

"Yes, Mother."

"And I want this nonsense with Thomas to stop."

Isabelle didn't respond.

"Did you hear me?"

"Yes."

"And?"

37

"And I'll move to Paris, marry him, and you'll never hear from me again." She glared back at her mother. "Is that what you want?"

Before her mother could respond, there was a sound outside that had them all cocking an ear.

"What the Devil is that?" asked her father first.

Her mother growled. "It better not be another fool asking us to come outside and hear some preacher while dinner is being prepared!"

Isabelle shivered as her heart hammered. "It sounds like something from church."

Her mother rose, heading for the front door. "Latin?"

Isabelle nodded, joining her mother as she opened the door.

She screamed.

Her father leaped to his feet, rushing to join them as Isabelle slowly backed away from a group of monks, all holding torches, approaching the doorway. She couldn't understand their words, she couldn't see their faces to see their lips moving, but they were chanting something in unison, something with words she recognized from the prayer services she attended every Sunday.

"What business do you have here?" demanded her father.

"Give us the one named Isabelle Leblanc."

Isabelle paled as her mother put a protective arm over her shoulders, the sound of her name spoken by so many in unison, sapping almost all her strength.

"What do you want with her? She's just a girl! Be off with you!"

Isabelle and her mother backed away from the door as the monks advanced, the Latin chant continuing, getting louder as they approached.

"Give us the one named Isabelle Leblanc," they repeated a second time as their prayer ended. It was a terrifying sound, and if she were to imagine what evil sounded like, it was this. The prayer repeated, several of the monks on the porch now, continuing to slowly walk forward. Her father slammed the door shut, dropping the bar in place. He backed away as the demand for her was repeated, followed by the hammering of what must have been fists on the door, then the entire front of their small home. Everything rattled from the pounding, and Isabelle screamed as a glass crashed onto the floor.

Her mother held her tight, the Lord's prayer rapidly recited in a whisper, and Isabelle sobbed as she joined in. They backed into the farthest corner from the door, her father with his arms stretched out, shielding them from whatever horrors lay on the other side as the chant continued, the voices of the monks rising with each repetition.

Then the door was kicked in, and as the monks streamed inside, crosses held in front of them, their faces cloaked in darkness, a blood-curdling scream erupted from someone, and it took her a moment before she realized it was her. Her father surged forward, his fists swinging, but he was quickly overwhelmed.

"Father!" she cried as her mother took his place, putting herself between her daughter and her assailants, yet she was no match for the powerful men who shoved her aside. Isabelle screamed as the monks grabbed her by the arms then the legs, lifting her up over their heads as she struggled against them. "Father! Help me!" She caught a glimpse of him as he reached for her, his forehead bloodied, his expression one of shame at not having protected her.

"Isabelle!" cried her mother, rushing toward her before being backhanded by one of the monks. The last glimpse Isabelle had of her was her poor mother crashing into the table and collapsing to the floor.

"Please! Let me go! I've done nothing wrong!"

She continued to struggle, then caught sight of someone whose very presence rocked her to her core.

Garnier, standing off to the side, his shoulders rounded inward, his chin buried in his chest.

As if he were ashamed of what he had done.

"Garnier! Help me! Please!"

But he said nothing, and he did nothing. Instead, he merely followed her, still held up in the air, over the heads of the monks who had stolen her from her family home.

She spotted others from the village lining the road and she struggled even harder. "Please, help me! They're taking me!"

And they too did nothing.

What is going on here?

"Why won't you help me? Please! I beg of you!"

She heard something ahead and raised her head to see a large fire in the center of the village, along with a crowd made of her neighbors and friends.

And she breathed a sigh of relief.

Surely, they'll put an end to this! Look how many there are!

She was lowered, then pushed to her knees in the cold snow, its icy chill swiftly making its presence felt as she was not dressed for the outdoors. Her eyes roamed the crowd as she pleaded for help, but instead, she was met with horrified stares.

What's happening?

A man approached in a long dark robe, his vestments unmistakable.

This was a priest. She reached out for him.

"Please, Father, help me! These men, they took me from my home! Please, Father, I've done nothing wrong!"

But he too said nothing, instead walking around her as she was held in place by two of the monks, the others having joined even more as they formed a larger circle around her, the torches and fire revealing a strange wagon nearby.

And she gasped at what was inside.

Women, all staring through the bars of the cage that held them, all as terrified as she was.

This makes no sense! What have I done?

"You see how beautiful she is," said the priest, still circling. "Her beauty is indeed uncommon." He stopped, suddenly jabbing a finger at her. "I say it is the work of the Devil himself!"

The crowd, her neighbors, gasped in shock, recoiling as if she were afflicted with some contagion. She struggled against the men holding her, realizing that no one here would help her. She was on her own, abandoned by the ones she had thought cared for her.

"See how she struggles? See how the demon inside is desperate to escape? For it knows its end is nigh, and that soon it will be cast back into the depths of Hell, once the exorcism is complete."

Demon? What was the man talking about? Did he think she was possessed somehow? She stopped her struggles, trying not to give him any excuse for his false impression, and forced as calm a voice as she could. "Please, Father, I'm not a demon. I'm not possessed. Please just let me go home to my family."

The priest laughed, shaking his head then turning to the crowd. "You see the trickery? First, she struggles and cries out, then she tries to fool us by being calm. This is the Devil himself at work, my good people, and he must be stopped."

Isabelle's heart sank as she realized there was nothing she could do. No matter how she acted, or what she said, it would be twisted into whatever he wanted.

But that wasn't what had her losing hope.

It was the reaction of those that surrounded them, the reaction on the faces of those she had known her entire life.

They believed him.

"But there is one last way we can prove it."

Isabelle watched as the priest went to the strange wagon. He reached inside and stepped back with a chain in his hand, then the strangest creature she had ever seen walked out of the cage, on all fours, yet upside down, her arms and legs twisted unnaturally as guttural grunts and barks erupted as she spat the vilest of things at the priest and the others.

She screamed in horror at what was obviously a beast from hell, no matter how much it might loosely resemble a woman. No person could move like that, no person could sound like that.

"See! It is as I said! They recognize each other! Your poor Isabelle recognizes the evil here, and knows that *I* recognize it! The demon inside her knows that its time has come!"

The thing on the chain rushed toward her, crawling like an upturned spider, if that were at all possible, a strange language shouted at her in a voice far too deep to be human. Isabelle recoiled, the grips on her arms tightening as she struggled to get away from whatever this thing was.

42

The priest pointed. "See, she speaks the tongue of demons to her fellow spirit. She would not do so if your beautiful Isabelle's soul had not been possessed." He spun dramatically to face the crowd, one hand held out with the chain restraining the creature, the other pointing to Isabelle. "But there is still time! I must take her to my church. Only there can I perform the exorcism and rid her of this evil that has taken over her body. Do I have your blessing, my good people?"

Fists pumped the air as shouts of approval surrounded her. She watched in horror as more joined in, and within moments everyone she had ever known or loved was shouting, "Save her! Save her!"

"Please, no! There's nothing wrong with me! He's wrong!" She struggled against the monks holding her to no avail. "Please! You know me!"

One of the monks took the chain held by the priest and led the creature back into the wagon as those holding Isabelle dragged her toward the prison on wheels. She was shoved into the back, stumbling forward and falling into the mess that was the floor of the wagon. She struggled to turn back for the door, but it was slammed shut and locked. She pushed to the bars, shoving her head through as the monks tossed their torches onto the fire, the crowd still chanting their support.

Tears rolled down her cheeks at the betrayal, and the priest's final words were lost on her. He climbed onto the front of the wagon and they began to move, the monks, now on horseback, surrounding them. She spotted Garnier and reached out for him.

"Please, Garnier! Help me!"

But again, he did nothing, only shame on his face.

Then he abruptly turned and darted into the darkness, her last hope gone.

De Rancourt Residence

Crécy-la-Chapelle, Kingdom of France

"So, are you thinking of leaving the Order?"

David glanced at Jeremy then returned his attention to shoveling the never-ending supply of dung from the animals and his friend. "I don't know. What do you think?"

Jeremy shrugged. "I don't know either. A year ago, it never would have even occurred to me to leave. I love being a Templar. I love my brothers. And one day I hoped to be a sergeant."

David paused, staring at his friend. "Really? We both could be sergeants by now, but instead, we both chose to remain with Sir Marcus long ago."

Jeremy frowned then tossed some hay onto the cleaned floor. "I suppose you're right. I guess we did give up our ambitions years ago."

"Ambition is a sin."

Jeremy leaned on his pitchfork. "Is it? I can never remember them all."

David grunted. "Perhaps then you wouldn't have passed the test to become sergeant."

Jeremy lunged playfully at him with the pitchfork. "Like you'd have done any better."

David threatened his friend with a load of cow patties, Jeremy wisely surrendering. "I've always been happy serving Sir Marcus. It's been so long, I know no different, and honestly, I don't want to know any different."

"But things have changed."

"You're right, they have. Not in my desire to serve our master, of course, but does serving him mean I have to remain within the Order?"

Jeremy shrugged. "What if the master is called back to duty? You wouldn't be able to accompany him."

David's eyebrows rose. "I suppose you're right. Though do you think he might be?"

Jeremy shrugged again. "I don't know. It's possible though. And remember the privileges. How many times have we availed ourselves of Templar outposts over the past months? You would no longer have access to these things, which means you wouldn't be as useful to our master."

David's eyes widened as he thought of how much he still relied on the brotherhood he had devoted his life to, and how much that brotherhood, and his access to its services, helped his master. He sighed. "It would have been nice to have a wife, I think."

Jeremy frowned. "I think there are aspects that could be fun, shall we say, but I've never understood women, nor do I desire to. Have you heard them down there? They never stop talking! They never stop ordering us around. Would you want that every hour of the day, just so you could bounce on top of them at night?"

David chuckled. "And I've heard that they don't always let you unless they're in the mood."

"Really? I thought Father Fischer in Acre always said that women's sole purpose was to tempt man, and they used sex as their weapon to draw us away from our vows."

David shrugged. "How would he know? He took the same vows as us."

Jeremy pursed his lips. "I've always wondered about that. How—"

"Help! Help! Anyone! I need help!"

David dropped his pitchfork and rushed out of the barn, Jeremy on his heels, and peered into the darkness. He spotted a dark figure on the snow at the bottom of the hill, waving his arms frantically as he stumbled and fell, struggling to regain his feet. "That *has* to be Garnier."

"They've taken Isabelle!"

David and Jeremy exchanged glances then rushed down the hill. The door to the home opened, Lady Joanne appearing in the doorway. "What's the meaning of this? Don't you realize the hour? Like I've already said, we have no intention of hearing some priest when there are children to be fed!"

David wasn't sure what she was talking about. Evidently, there had been visitors earlier he wasn't aware of, and judging from Garnier's state, one thing likely had nothing to do with the other. He grabbed the panicking boy by the shoulders. "What is it? What happened to

Isabelle?"

"I did a terrible thing! Oh God, I'm so sorry! I didn't mean to! I was just so angry over what she said."

Lady Joanne pulled them all inside and out of the cold. "Never mind that. What happened?"

"There was a priest and these monks. He was looking for people possessed by demons."

Lady Joanne shoved the boy into a chair then sat across from him. "You mean an exorcist? Is that what Rene was on about earlier when he was trying to get us to come with him?"

Garnier shrugged. "I don't know what an exorcist is."

"It doesn't matter. What happened to Isabelle?"

"He said that beautiful women could be possessed, and asked if there were any in the village who were both beautiful and acting differently. In my embarrassed state, I did something horrible."

David grabbed him by the shoulder, shoving him back in his chair. "What did you do?"

"I-I named her."

Joanne and Beatrice both gasped. Beatrice grabbed him by the hair, hauling him closer to her. "How could you do that, you stupid little fool!"

"I'm sorry! As soon as her name was out of my mouth, I knew I had gone too far, but then everyone started to agree that she could be possessed."

Joanne folded her arms. "I can't believe that. So, what happened?"

"They made me take them to her house. They took her then put her in the back of a strange wagon, one with an enclosed cage made of metal bars, I think."

David's jaw dropped. "You mean they've actually taken her with them?"

Garnier nodded, tears streaking his face. "Yes. She's gone."

"How long ago?"

"Not long. As long as it took me to run here from the center of the village and explain it to you."

David turned to Jeremy. "Three horses, minimal provisions, just weapons."

"Five minutes." Jeremy sprinted out the door, the mastiff Tanya following.

"Which direction did they go?"

"South."

"How many?"

"How many what?"

David swatted him on the back of the head. "How many men?"

Garnier cowered, holding up his hands. "I'm not sure. A dozen maybe? They were all dressed as monks, but they weren't like any monks I've ever seen. They attacked Mr. and Mrs. Leblanc. Monks wouldn't do that, would they?"

David shook his head. "No, I wouldn't think so. Where did they say they were taking her?"

"The priest said he was taking them to his church, then they'd be returned after he had performed some ritual to remove the demons possessing them."

"Them?"

"Yes, there were others in the wagon."

"How many?"

48

"I have no idea. At least several."

"And he said they would be returned when he was done with them?"

Garnier's face brightened. "Yes! Yes, it's true! That's a good thing, right? I mean, it means they don't intend to harm her?"

David pursed his lips. "Let's hope so, but there's still the matter of her abduction. We have to get her back, and I'm not so sure they'll agree to that." He stopped himself from cursing. "At least a dozen?"

"Yes."

David shook his head. "Then I don't see how we can do anything but try and reason with them."

"Horses are ready!"

David hauled Garnier to his feet. "You're coming with us."

Garnier appeared horrified at the suggestion. "Wh-why?"

"Because this is your fault. You need to tell them that you were wrong."

Garnier nodded, his entire body trembling as David shoved him out the door. Tanya growled at the young man, her keen senses telling her who was the source of all the commotion. David pointed inside. "Stay here. Guard the women and children."

Tanya stared up at him, panting.

"Inside. Now."

She dropped her head and obeyed, though was clearly not pleased about it.

David mounted his horse and turned to Lady Joanne. "We'll be back as soon as we can. If something goes wrong and we don't, get word to Sir Marcus and tell him everything you just heard."

Joanne reached up and squeezed his arm. "You be safe, and bring that sweet girl home."

"We'll do our best."

David urged his horse forward, and within moments the three of them were at a full gallop and off the property. They charged through the center of the village, a large fire in the middle of the road being pulled apart by some of the villagers, clearly some sort of event having occurred here recently.

If only Lady Joanne had sent one of us to hear this priest!

They charged past, some of the villagers stopping to stare, and he resisted the urge to chastise them for what they had all allowed to happen. The full moon and clear sky lit the way nicely, allowing them to keep a good pace, and within minutes, he spotted a group on horseback. He squinted in the dim light then cursed at the sight of a prisoner transport ahead.

"Halt!" he shouted, charging past the men on horseback then blocking their path, Jeremy and Garnier on either side of him. "I demand you release our friend, Isabelle Leblanc."

A man driving the wagon leaned forward, lit by two torches, one on either side of him, mounted to the wagon. "I'm afraid I can't do that."

David grabbed his bow and had it fitted with an arrow almost instantly, Jeremy doing the same, Garnier merely trembling beside him. "I must insist."

The sound of a dozen swords being drawn had sweat trickling down David's back as the monks revealed themselves to be unlike any he had encountered.

"You are outnumbered, my friend."

David lowered his bow. Slightly. "What kind of monks carry

weapons?"

"The kind that deal with demons, and those that would follow them."

"Demons? What are you talking about?"

"Your friend Isabelle, who your friend here suggested might be possessed, is indeed so. I intend to save her."

Garnier, to his credit, urged his horse forward slightly. "I-I made a mistake. I'm sorry, but I was hurt by something she had said earlier today. I didn't mean to get anyone hurt. I take back everything I said."

The priest leaned forward. "She hurt you?"

Garnier stared at the man, tears in his eyes. "Yes. But only with words. It was nothing."

"Don't you see that this is the work of the Devil? You like her, you adore her, yet she spurns you. And though she makes her lack of interest clear, her beauty continues to draw you in, and even now, after she has cut you with her words as deeply as a blade might stab you in the heart, you defend her. Don't you see the grip she has on you? Don't you see the grip the demon that possesses her has on your soul as well?" The priest shook his head. "No, your Isabelle has been lost to you. I will save her, and I promise you, she will be returned to you shortly, the Isabelle you once knew and loved. And perhaps then, she might be willing to give you her heart, for you will have been the one to save her through your courage in naming her."

Garnier stared at David helplessly. It was obvious the boy was having doubts, which was understandable. The priest was saying everything the young man wanted to hear. David examined the monks, assessing their level of experience by the way they held their swords, and he wasn't certain. He doubted they had the skills of a true warrior, yet they were a dozen strong. There was little hope of defeating them.

"Where are you taking her?" he asked.

"My church."

"And where is that?"

"I can't say. If its location fell into the wrong hands, then all could be lost." The priest leaned forward, his expression softening. "I can tell you all care deeply for this woman, and I appreciate that. If you love her, then you must let me save her. I swear to God that I mean her no harm. She will be cleansed of the evil that possesses her, and when the ritual is complete, she will be returned to you by my faithful servants. I swear to you that this is true."

David frowned, exchanging a glance with Jeremy, who seemed ready to take them all on, despite the odds. David shook his head slightly, and Jeremy growled in frustration.

"Now, please, my sons, move aside so I can continue my work. The sooner my travels are over, the sooner I can save your friend."

They had no choice. Continuing to challenge these men might result in a fight they couldn't win, and could result in the death of Isabelle. It was something they couldn't risk.

"Very well, Father." David gestured for the others to follow his lead as he guided his horse to the side of the road.

"Thank you, my sons. You will see your friend again soon."

The procession continued, the monks sheathing their swords, and as the wagon passed them, David's heart broke as he spotted their friend, her pleas for help tearing at his soul.

"I can't believe you're letting them go!"

David turned to Jeremy, blocking him with his arm. "We had no choice. They were over a dozen, and we are but three."

"But we have to do something."

"We will. I want you to follow them while I let Sir Marcus know what has happened." David grabbed Jeremy by the arm before he could take off after their friend. "And whatever you do, don't be seen. It could mean Isabelle's death. And yours."

Paris, Kingdom of France

"Was your meeting as boring as my waiting for you was?"

Sir Marcus glanced at his sergeant. "You were bored?"

Simon grunted. "Oh, no, not at all. Sitting in a room waiting for you for hours was simply thrilling."

"You could have filled your time with prayer."

Simon frowned. "Even I can only do that for so long." He sighed. "I find it hard to do alone. In the Holy Land, I always had our brothers to pray with. It felt more meaningful, like I was part of a community."

"You still are, just a different one."

Simon eyed him for a moment. "Yes, I realize that. And you know I enjoy praying with you and the squires, but you weren't in the room now, were you?"

Marcus continued to have a little fun at his sergeant's expense. "The

Lord was with you."

Simon shook his head. "Now I know you're being an ass."

Marcus tossed his head back, laughing. "You are so easy to annoy, my friend." He punched him gently on the shoulder. "I'll tell you what. Next time, you stay at the farm, and I'll do this monthly visit by myself."

Simon shook his head. "And give up an opportunity to get away from the smell of shit and squires? Absolutely not. I'll come, though next time leave me outside where I can at least watch the common people and remind myself why I hate this city."

Marcus looked about him at the simple people going about their business, few out now that the sun had set. "It's not that bad a place. These are good people in their own way. Not everyone can be as pious as those in the Order."

Simon pointed to an alleyway where some unsavory business between a man and a woman was underway. "This city is filled to the brim with depravity. How much good have we actually seen in all our visits? I dare say almost none."

"The Holy Land wasn't much better, my friend. We were simply shielded from much of it because of who we were, and how we lived."

Simon grunted. "The world would be a better place without all these sinners."

Marcus frowned. "I fear if we were to rid the world of all sinners, there'd be few people left."

Simon was about to respond when he stopped, pointing ahead. "Fire."

Marcus urged his horse forward, Simon directly behind him, and within moments they had the building in sight. And Marcus' heart sank. It was their destination, the home of their friend Thomas Durant, the current suitor to Isabelle Leblanc. He spotted Thomas on the roof, desperately throwing snow on the flames, the thatched roof proving to be kindling.

Marcus charged forward and stood on his saddle, leaping into the air and grabbing onto the edge of the roof. He swung his legs up then rolled onto the building, rushing over to Thomas' side.

"Sir Marcus! What are you doing here?"

"Never mind that. Tear it out and throw it over the edge." He grabbed a bundle of the flaming straw and tore it free, tossing it over the edge. "Simon, make sure this doesn't spread!"

"Yes, sir!" came his friend's voice from below.

Thomas changed his tactics, and together with Marcus, they had torn out the affected area within about ten minutes of exhausting effort. Thomas flopped onto his back, Marcus doing the same, both their chests heaving.

"What happened?" asked Marcus as he caught his breath.

"Someone is jealous of my success, I guess."

Marcus sat up. "But it's been months. Why now?"

Thomas shrugged. "I don't know." He sighed. "Well, maybe I know. It was old man Caron, I'm sure. His granddaughter disappeared, and he thinks I can help find her. When I told him I couldn't, he got angry. He knows I work for Mrs. Thibault, and he's convinced she has something to do with her disappearance."

Marcus frowned at the mention of the vile woman's name, Simone Thibault having taken over her husband's business when he died, now a parasite that dealt in all things nefarious, not the least of which was lending money to desperate people at exorbitant rates of interest.

"Does she?"

Thomas shrugged. "I don't know. I've learned not to ask such questions."

"Where does this old man live?"

"Just down the street. The house with a red and white gable."

Marcus rose, holding out a hand for Thomas. "Perhaps it's best if I had a word with him so this doesn't happen again."

Thomas took the hand and Marcus pulled him to his feet. "That might be a good idea. I'm going to try and fix this roof. It looks like snow tonight."

Marcus nodded. "I'll be back shortly." He swung down from the roof to find Simon stomping out the last of the straw they had tossed over the edge. "I have to pay those responsible a visit. Give him a hand, would you?"

"Are you sure you don't want me to come with you?"

"I think I can handle an old man by myself."

"He might have sons."

"If he does, I'll send them over to help with the repairs you so obviously don't want to be involved with."

Simon grinned. "You know me so well."

Enclos du Temple, Templar Fortress
Paris, Kingdom of France

It had been a foolish ride, but there had been no time to waste. Crécy-la-Chapelle was several hours ride from Paris, less at a full gallop, though doing so in the dark in winter was imprudent. It was late, though still before midnight when he arrived, the short winter days throwing everything off.

The days in the Holy Land never seemed so short.

But it was still late, and the only man who might know where he could find Sir Marcus, who evidently wasn't staying at the Templar barracks here, had already retired for the night.

As he waited impatiently, his toe tapping rapidly, he found his thoughts turning to Jeremy, and prayed that the fool didn't let his temper or impulsiveness get him into trouble.

I should have been the one to follow them.

But he was a better rider than Jeremy, and speed was of the essence. Sir Marcus would know what to do, and he had little doubt that the four of them together could best a dozen inexperienced monks in battle, especially if he and Jeremy thinned them out a little from a distance.

A door opened at the far end of the grand hall he was waiting in, and he leaped to his feet as he recognized the regalia of the Templar Master for France, Sir Matthew Norris, the most senior member of the Order within the Kingdom.

"Why have I been disturbed?"

David bowed deeply. "I apologize, sir, it is my fault. I have an urgent message for Sir Marcus de Rancourt, and no one seems to know where he is."

The man's anger ebbed slightly. "I met with Sir Marcus earlier today. He didn't stay with us?"

David shook his head. "I'm afraid not, sir."

"He made mention of visiting a friend after our meeting. Perhaps he is there."

"Did he mention a name?"

Sir Norris shook his head. "No, I'm afraid not."

David's mind raced as he ran through the short list of whom Marcus might know in the city, and that would be willing to let him through their door without killing him. He smiled. "Thomas Durant. It must be him."

Norris' eyes narrowed. "I know that name." He held up a hand, cutting off David's explanation. "Why the urgency?"

"A friend has been kidnapped."

Norris frowned. "That's most unfortunate. By whom?"

"A priest who claims she has been possessed by a demon, and an exorcism must be performed."

"And is your friend possessed?"

David's jaw dropped. "Most definitely not!"

"And you were unable to stop her abduction?"

David shook his head. "No. He was accompanied by a dozen armed monks."

Norris' eyebrows shot up. "Armed monks?"

David nodded. "Yes, sir."

"When you find your master, return here with him, no matter the hour. I may have news that can help."

"I will. Thank you, sir."

Norris dismissed him with a flick of the wrist before heading for the door whence he came. David remained bowing until it shut, then rushed outside to his horse, wondering what news Norris might have that would warrant waking him up yet again.

But that was for Marcus to worry about.

Please, Lord, let him be with Thomas.

Caron Residence
Paris, Kingdom of France

"What business does a Templar Knight have in our humble home?"

Marcus bowed at the old man who had remained seated upon his arrival. It was a wretchedly humble home, as most were in this area, and he knew from a previous visit to Thomas', that he was making long-overdue repairs to his family home that could indeed make the neighbors jealous of his newfound success.

This house appeared to be bursting at the seams with people, at least three families and as many generations apparently living under the one roof.

"I've come to speak to you about what happened tonight to Master Thomas Durant's home."

Caron spat on the floor at the mention of the name. "And what is he to you?"

"A friend." Marcus stepped slightly closer. "A *good* friend. And someone who has no quarrel with you." He held up a finger, cutting off any response. "Tell me of your granddaughter."

One of the sons, lined up behind their father, stepped forward. "It's my daughter, Yvette. She's been missing several days. Nobody has seen her."

Marcus folded his arms. "I'm sorry for what has happened, and I understand why you are all upset, but burning Thomas' house wasn't necessary, and accomplished nothing."

The old man grunted. "It got *you* here, didn't it?"

Marcus' eyebrows rose slightly. "And what could I possibly do about it?"

The old man shrugged. "I don't know, but you're a Templar Knight. Surely you can do more than any of us could."

Marcus frowned. The man was right, though what he could possibly do, he had no idea. But he had to tell them something. "I'll inform Command what has happened, and I know they'll listen for any word on your granddaughter, but beyond that, there's not much I can do." He turned to the father. "What does she look like?"

"A tiny little thing, long blond hair. Quite beautiful."

Marcus smiled at the man. "She sounds lovely. I hope you find her."

The wind howled outside, shaking the house.

"Now, I must ask you a favor. Master Thomas' roof is damaged badly, and a storm is approaching. I would like your sons to help us repair it before it is too late."

The grandfather rose, extending his hand. "If you promise to help us find my granddaughter, then you'll have all the help you need."

62

Marcus shook the man's hand. "I will do everything within my power."

"May the good Lord help guide you to our precious Yvette."

Marcus stepped out into the cold, the wind making its presence known, the sons following with their tools. And as they trudged toward Thomas' home, Marcus was left to worry that even if he kept the promise he had just made, it would mean little.

He feared Yvette might be lost to the depravity that was Paris.

Durant Residence

Paris, Kingdom of France

As David rounded the last bend leading to Thomas' house, he pulled up short, his mouth agape. A crew of men was working on the roof, and there was evidence of a fire. He couldn't make out who the men were, but it was obvious they were working furiously to beat the impending storm he was feeling in his bones.

One of the workers cursed and David grinned, recognizing Simon's voice. And if Simon was here, then Sir Marcus must be as well. He searched the darkness and spotted his master standing across the road, leaning against a hitching post, deep in thought.

"Sir!"

Marcus stood straight, striding rapidly toward him, concern on his face as David dismounted. "David, what are you doing here? Is everything all right at the farm?"

David shook his head. "No, sir, it's terrible. Isabelle has been taken by some priest. He claims that she's possessed by a demon, and he intends to perform an exorcism on her."

"You let him take her?"

"Oh, God, no! We didn't know. That Garnier boy that's sweet on her told us and we gave chase, but he was accompanied by a dozen monks, all armed. We challenged them, but they refused to give her up."

"Where is she now?"

David sighed. "I don't know, but Jeremy is following them at a distance. He's to get word back to us when he can."

Marcus turned toward Thomas' house. "Simon! A word!"

"Thank God!" muttered the sergeant as he climbed down to the street. He stretched. "Just when I was starting to enjoy myself." His eyes narrowed when he spotted David. "What are you doing here? What's wrong?"

Marcus beckoned him closer. "Isabelle has been taken."

Simon's eyes shot wide. "What? By who?"

"A priest and a dozen *armed* monks, if David is to be believed."

David's jaw dropped. "Surely you don't think—"

Marcus held up a hand, cutting him off. "Of course, I believe you, though I still can't believe it, if you know what I mean."

David sighed with relief at the misunderstanding. "Yes, I do. If I hadn't seen it with my own eyes, I never would have believed it. Monks with swords! It's un-Christian!"

Simon grunted. "We're monks."

David stared at him. "Yes, but with special dispensation from the

Pope, something I'm sure they don't have."

Marcus brought the conversation back on track. "Did they give a reason?"

"For taking Isabelle?"

"No, for being armed. Surely you questioned them on this departure from the norm."

David nodded. "I did, of course. The priest said that they needed to defend themselves against demons and those who would serve them, or some such nonsense."

Marcus pursed his lips then sighed loudly. "A perfectly plausible explanation." He tapped his chin. "Do we know why she was taken? I mean, why the priest thought she was possessed?"

"According to Garnier, it was his fault. Apparently, the priest had asked if there was anyone possessed in the village, and that a sign of that might be uncommon beauty, saying it was the Devil's work. The boy was jealous or angry about something he had overheard, something said by Isabelle in the presence of Lady Joanne and Beatrice, and he named her in a fit of rage."

Simon cursed. "Surely that wasn't enough for the priest to accept that she was possessed!"

"No, Garnier outdid himself. He told the priest that she had been acting differently since we arrived, and there was a suggestion that perhaps we brought some sort of evil back with us from the Holy Land that then possessed her."

Simon threw up his arms. "Unbelievable!"

Marcus agreed. "Yet so ridiculously so, that it sounds plausible to those who would be blinded by fear." He looked at David. "And what did our fellow villagers do?"

David's cheeks flushed with rage. "Apparently urged them on! Can you believe it? They've known her since the day she was born, yet with a few words, are willing to believe she is the Devil's servant and should be taken away to have God knows what done to her!"

Marcus sighed. "We've seen it in the Holy Land on too many occasions. All it takes is one accusation, genuine or false, to destroy a life." He squared his shoulders. "We must seek her out immediately."

David suddenly remembered the Templar Master's request. "Before we do, Sir Norris asked me to bring you back before you left. He might have information that could help us."

Marcus nodded. "Then prepare our horses. I have to tell Thomas what has transpired. I'm afraid this will break his heart."

Durant Residence

Paris, Kingdom of France

Thomas worked in awkward silence with Mr. Caron's sons as they repaired the roof the old man had damaged in his anger. The only words uttered, by the eldest, had been an appreciation of the fact their father was able to toss a torch that high. It was impressive since this was a two-story construction, but anger could sometimes give someone strength they wouldn't normally have.

And at the moment, he had no rage in him.

He understood why Mr. Caron had done what he had. He was worried about his granddaughter. As he should be. Thomas wasn't sure what he'd do if faced with a similar situation. He liked to imagine he'd do everything in his power, and that if he found whoever had taken that person so close to him, he'd tear out their throat with his bare hands.

But he wasn't that type of person. If he were to describe himself in one word, he'd say meek. Others might say worse, especially now that there were jealousies at play. When his father had been alive, plying his trade as an expert forger, creating documents for rich and poor alike that could fool even the King's officials, there had been little money for luxuries. They were always fed just enough, they were always warm just enough, but there was rarely a full belly or a bead of sweat known in the Durant household.

Now all of that had changed.

After his father's murder, which had left him alone and starving, he had been saved by Sir Marcus and his men, and through circumstance, gained employment with a most wretched soul who paid well. Too well. It made it almost impossible to leave her employ no matter how desperately he wanted to. He kept defending himself, to himself, by saying he wasn't doing anything truly bad. He merely tallied the numbers. He never forced anyone to pay their debts, in fact, he rarely saw any of the debtors.

He was a numbers man, math, along with reading and writing, skills his father had passed down to him, and all he had to offer to the world. He wasn't a strong man, not particularly skilled at anything manual. He glanced at the three sons, working at his side, and was shamed by how swiftly and ably they worked.

They were men.

He wasn't.

They have fifteen years at least on you.

Perhaps in time he'd fill out, become strong, become skilled at things such as roof repair, as he gained more experience and muscle on his bones, but he doubted it. He had always thrived when using his brain. Unfortunately, in this part of Paris, there was little need for brains, and the only steady work was given to those who affiliated themselves with one of the many criminal organizations in the area, who took a generous cut of anything earned.

He had always refused, yet here he was, working for one of those gangs, tallying those shares of salaries hard earned on the backs of others desperate for work.

You're pathetic.

"Master Thomas, I must speak with you!"

He leaned over the edge of the roof and saw Sir Marcus beckoning him. He climbed down and brushed off before presenting himself to the man who had offered him a home, and to whom he had refused the offer. He still thought it was the right choice, though with the blooming romance with Isabelle, he was thinking moving to the farm might be a wise decision.

If not inevitable.

His eyes narrowed as he noticed Marcus' grave expression. "What's wrong?" He spotted David standing with Simon and frowned.

Shouldn't he be at the farm?

His jaw dropped. "Something's happened to Isabelle, hasn't it?"

Marcus nodded. "Yes. She's been taken."

He felt a rush of blood from his head and reached out for the wall to steady himself. "By whom?"

"A priest who claims she has been possessed by a demon, or some such nonsense."

He drew a deep breath, recovering his balance. "We must find her!"

"And we will. We are heading back to the Fortress now, then will immediately begin looking for her. Jeremy is tracking her, so we *will* find her. We just need to find him."

Thomas stood as tall as he could, squaring his shoulders in an effort to look more of a man than he was. "I must go with you."

Marcus nodded. "Of course. We'll collect you when we're done at the Fortress. That way, you'll be able to finish your roof repairs."

"Forget the roof. Isabelle is more important."

"I agree, but there's nothing you can do to help her at this moment. Take care of your home, and we will be back in short order. I'll leave David here to help."

Thomas sighed. "Fine, you're right, of course." He frowned. "And I guess I should send word to Mrs. Thibault that I will be away."

Marcus gripped Thomas' shoulder. "You do that. I'll be back shortly."

Enclos du Temple, Templar Fortress
Paris, Kingdom of France

"You have no messages for me?"

The sergeant manning the front desk shook his head. "I'm sorry, Sir Marcus, none have arrived for you. Nor any for your sergeant or squire."

Marcus sighed. "That's unfortunate, though not unexpected. I guess we'll have to go looking for him. We'll need four fresh horses, provisioned for two days' journey."

The sergeant snapped his fingers and a squire emerged from the shadows. "You heard him."

"Yes, sergeant!" The boy rushed through a set of doors toward the stables to fulfill the order without another word.

The sergeant turned back to Marcus. "Do you have any idea where he might be?"

"All we know is that he was last heading south out of Crécy-la-Chapelle, but that was hours ago, early evening. It's almost midnight now."

"I can have a message sent to all of our outposts in the area to have our personnel watch for him."

"Do that, though I'm sure he'll avail himself of any of our brothers he might encounter."

"And should he be found, where do you want the message sent?"

"Send it to all the outposts in the area. We'll check in regularly during our search."

"Very well."

"Belay that."

Marcus turned to see Sir Norris, the Templar Master for the Kingdom of France, swiftly striding toward them. Marcus bowed deeply, as did Simon. "Sir, I must apologize for the late hour."

Norris waved his hand, dismissing the apology. "No need to apologize, it was I who told your squire to have you report to me." He turned to his sergeant. "Have any message for Sir Marcus sent here. I think he will be remaining in the city for at least the night."

Marcus' eyes narrowed. "Sir?"

Norris turned back toward the door, beckoning Marcus to follow. "Come with me. I have a private matter to discuss with you."

Marcus hesitated. "My sergeant?"

Norris glanced over his shoulder, eyeing Simon. "No doubt you'll tell him regardless."

Simon grinned and followed, closing the door behind him as they were offered seats in Norris' office.

Norris sat on the edge of his desk. "What I'm about to tell you is of a delicate nature, and few know of it."

Marcus leaned forward with anticipation.

"About a week ago, the daughter of Lord Allard was kidnapped, her guards murdered. Her chaperone, however, survived, and told of a priest and a group of monks who might have been involved."

Marcus' eyebrows shot up and he exchanged an excited glance with Simon. "That sounds too similar to be a coincidence. What else can you tell us?"

"Not much, I'm afraid. The report I had was very brief. The Court has asked us to keep a lookout for anything throughout the Kingdom, and we have agreed to help in the search, as Lord Allard is a friend to the Order, one of the few we have in King Philip's court."

Simon shifted in his chair. "I find it difficult to believe these two abductions could be related. Lord Allard's daughter is nobility. Isabelle Leblanc is a simple farm girl."

Norris nodded. "While I agree they seem impossible to link, it was the mention of a priest accompanied by monks, armed monks, that made me think they might be connected."

Marcus scratched his chin. "While I find it almost impossible to believe they are connected intentionally, I too find it too much of a coincidence to ignore the possibility."

"Agreed."

"With your permission, we'll talk to Lord Allard and the survivor. They might have valuable information."

"Do that."

Marcus rose, quickly followed by Simon. "Oh, one more thing, sir.

THE TEMPLAR DETECTIVE AND THE UNHOLY EXORCIST

Have you heard of any other abductions in the city?"

Norris' eyes narrowed. "Why?"

"Well, a friend of ours who lives nearby, said a young woman is missing, a quite beautiful girl, and I'm wondering if there is a pattern here."

Norris sighed, shaking his head. "I hate to say this, but I've been in Paris a long time, and I've lived in other large cities before this. Unfortunately, beautiful young women disappearing is not a rarity."

"But why would they be taken?"

"I'm afraid we must assume they have been taken for carnal reasons, or other sinful purposes. It is a blight on our society that these things happen, and we can only pray that your friend Isabelle, Lord Allard's daughter, and your friend's neighbor, were taken for other, less depraved reasons."

Marcus frowned. "I fear the worst. Was Lord Allard's daughter comely?"

"I believe she was."

Marcus tensed. "If she was kidnapped by the same person who took Isabelle, then I fear it is likely they have been abducted for the same reason, and that has nothing to do with demonic possession."

Lord Allard's Residence

Paris, Kingdom of France

"Please, we must see your master. We might have information on his daughter."

The man stared through the Judas hole at Marcus, the distrusting eyes and annoyed expression unchanged. "And what might that be?"

Marcus shook his head. "I'm afraid that is for Lord Allard's ears only."

"He and her Ladyship are in prayer, and cannot be disturbed. Unless you actually have their missing daughter with you, I cannot let you enter."

The Judas hole snapped shut and Marcus slammed a fist against the thick gate blocking their way.

Simon cursed. "Now what?"

Marcus mounted his horse, staring at the large estate that perhaps contained valuable answers to the myriad of questions he had. "We must speak with him somehow."

"Not if that little troll has anything to say about it."

Marcus thought for a moment then turned his horse around. "I have an idea."

Simon grunted. "You always do. Care to share?"

"Sir Denys de Montfort lives not far from here. As a member of the court, perhaps he'll have more sway than us."

Simon nodded. "It's worth a try, I suppose. But wouldn't he still be considered a disgrace after that affair?"

Marcus shrugged. "Perhaps. I'm not one to keep up with the goings on at the King's Court, though I'm certain no matter his current situation, he will see us, and at a minimum, be able to advise us." He stared up at the sky, the clouds thickening, the stars already gone, the moon fading. "Let's hurry. It's getting very late and that storm is getting close."

A short gallop had them at Sir Denys' home, this neighborhood on the finer side of the Seine, home to much of the aristocracy that ruled the Kingdom of France. There was more wealth here than he had ever seen, areas like this rare in the Holy Land, or at least in the realms he patrolled.

As expected, they were quickly shown in, but the man they were presented to was a pale imitation of the proud man they had met only months before. Seated behind his desk, disheveled and evidently soaked in alcohol, Sir Denys brightened slightly at their arrival. He rose, stumbling and almost losing his feet before catching himself with a well-placed hand.

He hiccupped.

"I must apologize for my condition. If I had known you were coming, I would have made certain I was presentable."

Marcus strode forward and shook the man's hand. "No need to apologize." He eyed the man for a moment. "May I ask if you are well? You appear…"

"A mess? An embarrassment?" Denys gestured toward two chairs then dropped back into his own. "While things may have ended well for you and your friends, I nearly lost everything, despite being innocent and having helped bring the perpetrators to justice."

Simon grunted. "You *did* think you were having an affair with Lady Joanne."

Denys frowned. "Yeah, that's what they said." He sighed. "I managed to escape with my lands and title, but little else. Certainly any respect has been lost." He cursed. "It's ridiculous. If the public only knew the level of depravity that occurs among the Court, there would likely be a revolution, and the entire lot of them would find themselves beheaded."

Marcus folded his arms. "I'm sure you're correct."

Denys apparently sensed some urgency in Marcus' demeanor. "I'm sorry, enough about me. What brings you here, my friends? Dare I hope that it is a simple visit?"

Marcus frowned. "I'm afraid not."

Denys sighed, clearly dejected. "I suspected as much. What can I do for you? Anything I have is yours. If it weren't for you, I would have probably been drawn and quartered. I owe you my life."

Marcus shook his head. "We were doing God's work. There is no debt owed."

"Of course you were." Denys straightened himself as best he could, though was still slightly off-kilter. "Tell me what I can do for you."

"You, of course, know Lord Allard?"

Denys' eyebrows rose slightly. "Of course, of course. He and I were good friends until the scandal. He, umm, like all my former friends, have distanced themselves from me." He grunted. "Until they need my vote, then we'll all be dining together soon enough."

"You heard of his daughter?"

"Annette? I did. A tragedy, though I know few details. Abducted on her way to their estate in Chantilly." Denys shook his head. "It's terrifying how unsafe the roads have become these days." His eyes narrowed. "But why do you ask? Have you become involved somehow?"

"It is an unfortunate possibility. You may have heard us speak of a young woman from Crécy-la-Chapelle named Isabelle?"

Denys nodded. "Yes, I believe so." He smiled. "If I'm to understand your squires, she has quite the thing for you."

Marcus shifted in his chair and Simon snickered. "Umm, that is, umm, no longer true. Another has caught her eye, thank God."

Denys laughed. "You Templars and your vows of celibacy. You don't know what you're missing."

Marcus shrugged. "One cannot miss what one has never had."

Denys regarded him for a moment. "I suppose that's true, though you might want to try it out to see what all the fuss is about!" He laughed again, his elbow slipping off his chair before a quick recovery, then became serious. "Something has happened to the young one, I fear?"

"Your fears would be justified. She has been abducted, and from the little we know, it may have been by the same people who kidnapped Lord Allard's daughter."

Denys' jaw dropped. "Surely not!"

"We must speak with Lord Allard if we are to be sure, and there is little time to waste, however he refuses to be seen."

Denys pounded a fist onto his desk. "If he knew, I assure you, he would."

Marcus agreed. "While that may be true, his man will not let us past the gate."

Denys rose, Marcus and Simon following. "Give me a few minutes to make myself presentable, and I will accompany you. Surely a member of the Court, no matter how disgraced, will be permitted entry."

Marcus bowed his head. "That was our hope."

Denys wobbled past, and Marcus reached out a steadying hand that the nobleman took for a brief moment, then waved off. "If I'm not back in ten minutes, you may need to come find me." He hiccupped again. "I may have, umm, succumbed."

Marcus watched the inebriated man leave the room, then started for the door after hearing a loud crash.

"I'm okay!"

Simon frowned. "Are we sure we want to show up with him? We may never be allowed to see Lord Allard."

Marcus sighed. "We have little choice. Let's just pray for the good Lord to sober him up enough for us to gain entry, then he can sleep it off for all I care."

Durant Residence
Paris, Kingdom of France

David and the others inspected their handiwork, and in his inexpert opinion, the roofing repair looked well executed. Thomas apparently agreed, thanking the three men who had been helping them before they all climbed down to the street below. Handshakes were exchanged.

"Thank you for your help," said Thomas, his voice low.

The eldest replied. "Our father was wrong in what he did, but he is a desperate man. We all are."

"If you hear anything about my daughter, you'll let us know?"

Thomas nodded at the youngest. "You have my word. And should *you* hear anything, let the Fortress know, and they'll send word to Sir Marcus."

"We will." The man sighed. "I don't know what I'll do if she doesn't come back. Yvette is all I have left. My wife is dead, as are all of our other children. Yvette and I were the only two to survive the sickness last year."

Thomas nodded. "It was a terrible time. So many died. But your daughter was strong enough to survive that, and I'm sure she's strong enough to survive whatever it is that has happened now. Continue to pray for her, and I'm sure if there is anything that can be done, Sir Marcus will be the one to do it."

The man gave Thomas a thumping hug then left with his brothers, leaving David to regard Thomas for a moment, impressed with the young man, something he couldn't remember feeling before. He was about to say something when two squires from the Fortress arrived, each on horseback, each leading two other fully provisioned horses.

"Squire David?"

David stepped forward. "Yes."

"As requested by Sir Marcus, four horses provisioned for two days' travel."

David and Thomas took the new arrivals by the reins and hitched them. "Tell your master that my master thanks him."

The squire bowed his head then turned his horse around, he and his companion quickly lost in the dark. David inspected the horses, always one to double-check the work of others, but found everything in order. He looked up at the sky, a wind howling now, a light dusting of snow blowing across the rooftops.

"I suspect we won't be going anywhere at this hour."

Thomas agreed. "What should we do?"

"We can't leave these horses like this. Let's strip them down and prepare them for the night. Should Sir Marcus want to leave, we can have them ready again in short order."

Thomas nodded then hesitated.

"What is it?"

"I'm thinking that perhaps I should see Mrs. Thibault while I can, in case we leave in a hurry."

"Will she see you at this hour?"

"That woman rarely sleeps."

David grunted. "Then that might be wise. We wouldn't want you getting in trouble with her." He began work on one of the horses. "You go, I'll manage by myself."

Thomas bowed slightly then bolted before David had a chance to suggest he take one of the horses to shorten the journey.

And they say he's a sharp one.

Lord Allard's Residence
Paris, Kingdom of France

Marcus' suspicions had been proven correct. Returning with a member of the Court, no matter the Court's current opinion of the man, had granted them swift entrance, though not a swift audience. It was easily another half an hour before Lord Allard appeared, and his expression suggested he was none too pleased to have visitors at this hour.

His displeasure increased severalfold when he spotted Denys. "Sir Denys, I hope you have a good explanation for this interruption. I'm certain you know our situation."

Denys bowed deeply. "And as your friend and humble servant, I must let you know you have my sympathies. I cannot imagine what you and your lovely wife are going through."

Allard was having none of it. "Of course you can't. You haven't any children. Nor will you ever if you continue on the way you have been."

Denys ignored the barb, instead bowing again. "You are right, of course, and I assure you that after recent events, I am a reformed man."

"I hope so. Now, what is it you want?"

Denys extended an arm toward Marcus and Simon. "You may remember Sir Marcus de Rancourt from his multiple, shall we say, *unscheduled* appearances at Court?"

Allard looked Marcus up and down. "I do. And what business does a Templar Knight have at my home during my hour of need?"

Marcus stepped forward, bowing his head. "Word has reached the Fortress of your daughter's plight, along with a few critical details of the abduction that bear a striking resemblance to another that happened just hours ago."

Any annoyance on Allard's face was wiped away, and he ushered them into chairs as he rounded his desk and sat. "Please, tell me everything."

"A friend of ours, a young woman named Isabelle Leblanc, was accused of being possessed by demons, and was taken by a priest, along with a group of monks."

Allard's eyes bulged and he gasped. "Monks!" He rose slightly. "Hercules!"

The door immediately opened.

"Get Emelisse at once."

"Yes, m'Lord."

Allard gestured for Marcus to continue as the door closed. "Please, continue."

"My squires gave chase as soon as they found out, demanded the release of our friend, but were stopped when the monks drew swords."

"Armed monks!" hissed Allard, his face flush with excitement. "This echoes much of what my daughter's escort has told us. A priest, accompanied by a group of monks who then attacked and killed the others then took my daughter. He spoke of saving her soul, or some such nonsense." He leaned back in his chair. "Frankly, I wasn't sure whether I believed her or not, but after hearing your story, I now fear I have wasted time in dismissing her account as the ravings of an injured woman."

"Injured?"

"She was left for dead, hit over the head with something. She's lucky to be alive. The scene of the abduction was discovered by a traveler who took possession of the carriage and rode it to the nearest town where a group of nuns was able to save her. I didn't know what had happened until she was lucid enough to send word to me of the attack. By then, days had passed, and there was no hope of finding my daughter."

The door opened and a woman entered, accompanied by another physically supporting her. She appeared near death, her head wrapped in bandages, one side of her face darkly bruised.

Marcus rose. "If I had known she was so injured, I would have gone to her."

Allard dismissed his concerns as if the woman's wellbeing was of no importance. Marcus offered her his chair, and she sat with a grateful though weak smile.

"This is Sir Marcus. Tell him what happened to my daughter."

Emelisse nodded, wincing at the movement. "We were on our way to the estate in Chantilly when we passed another carriage. It was some sort of transport. I didn't catch much more than a glimpse of it, as I was sitting on the opposite side from my mistress, but I thought I heard women in some distress."

Marcus' eyes narrowed. "Distress?"

"Yes. I'm certain I heard women crying, but I must have been mistaken. I did see the man, the driver, for a moment, and I'm quite certain he was a priest."

"Why would you say that?"

"His manner of dress. He also held up a cross, said something in Latin, then something like, 'Do not worry my child, your suffering will be over soon.'" She shuddered. "That was when the monks attacked us, killing the coachman and guard, and before it was over, I was hit by something from behind." She stole a quick glance at Allard. "I'm sorry, but I'm afraid I don't remember anything beyond that."

"And the men that attacked. You're sure they were monks?"

She shrugged. "I think so. They certainly appeared to be. They all had long dark robes with hoods that covered their heads." She frowned. "But they couldn't be, could they? Monks wouldn't murder in cold blood, would they?"

Simon grunted. "Apparently some do."

"Is there anything else you can tell us?"

She shook her head, again wincing. "I'm afraid not. I wish I could, I truly do."

Marcus smiled gently at her. "Very well. Please see to your health. If you think of anything, tell your master so he can get word to us."

"I will."

Her companion helped her up and they waited in silence for her to leave and the door to close.

Allard broke the silence. "What do you think?"

Marcus returned to his chair. "I think a priest claiming he's going to save your daughter's soul sounds an awful lot like the same priest claiming something similar in our case."

Denys agreed. "For me, it's the armed monks that clinches it."

Marcus nodded. "The question is, why was your daughter taken, and our friend taken." He paused, trying to figure out a delicate way to put his next question. "Forgive me, m'Lord, but your daughter, is she…beautiful?"

Allard frowned. "I'm not one to speak of such things. Is it important?"

"Yes, I believe it might be. Apparently, our priest spoke of uncommon beauty being the sign of the Devil's work. It was why our friend was taken. If your daughter…"

Allard sighed. "Yes, she is very beautiful. There is not a man in Paris who wouldn't pay handsomely to have her on his arm."

Marcus pursed his lips. "I think there can be no doubt it is the same man, but his purpose I question. I'm sorry to ask this, but did your daughter behave oddly in any way, any mannerisms that might make a priest think she could be possessed?"

Allard grunted. "Nonsense. She was a perfectly normal girl. And your friend?"

"The same." Marcus scratched his beard. "Why would a priest take these two completely different women? And kill to do so in your daughter's case?"

Simon scowled. "There's no way a holy man would do such a thing." He paused, his eyes widening. "Unless he isn't a priest."

Everyone turned their attention to the sergeant.

"What do you mean?" asked Allard. "That he's an imposter?"

Simon shifted in his seat. "Well, I mean, a priest kidnapping beautiful women, accompanied by a dozen armed monks? They could as easily be a dozen brigands with stolen robes, and he with equally questionably obtained vestments."

Marcus' head slowly bobbed at his sergeant's theory. "That is a possibility. It certainly makes more sense than a priest collecting possessed women to later perform exorcisms on, and who is willing to kill anyone trying to stop him." He paused then frowned. "I fear for young Jeremy."

Simon grunted. "Let's pray he doesn't do anything foolish."

Marcus turned to Allard. "We will do everything in our power to find your daughter, m'Lord."

Allard rose. "I shall pray for your success."

Marcus bowed then headed for the door before pausing. "I'm sorry, m'Lord. Your daughter's name?"

"Annette."

East of Paris, Kingdom of France

Isabelle sat huddled against the side of the wagon as the door at the rear was opened and a large bowl of food was tossed inside, carrots and other root vegetables bouncing on the floor. There was a mad scramble for the food, and by the time she realized what was happening, all had been taken.

Her stomach rumbled as those around her ate the uncooked vegetables as quickly as they could, as if scared whatever they had managed to grab might be snatched from them by one of the others. She watched the others eat, some clearly locked inside the cage longer than she, and instead focused on her warmth, drawing her knees up as far as she could and adjusting her clothing to cover as much of her body as possible against the frigid winter night.

She was hungry, but she had eaten well at lunch, and she estimated it was now just past midnight. The women around her, with the exception of the creature near the front of the wagon, seemed normal. Everyone was simply scared. Why this priest thought they were all possessed was beyond her. Could he see something in her soul that she couldn't? Could he recognize something she had no clue was there?

She had thought this was her punishment for hurting Garnier's feelings earlier this morning, but she had dismissed the notion. There was no possible way the Lord would punish her like this for a few poorly chosen words, especially when most of them were spoken by Lady Joanne and Beatrice.

Especially Beatrice.

But she wouldn't fit in here.

Isabelle paused at the thought. *Why* wouldn't Beatrice fit in here? She hadn't noticed until just now, but every woman around her, mostly filthy and unkempt from the conditions, would in any other circumstance be considered quite beautiful. In fact, the girl sitting beside her was wearing clothing so fine, though soiled, that she imagined she could be a princess, or certainly nobility.

The woman noticed her looking at her, then broke the carrot she was tightly gripping in two, offering her the other half. Isabelle smiled, but shook her head. "No, you eat it. You look hungrier than me." She leaned in slightly closer. "Tomorrow, though, I might take you up on the offer."

The girl flashed a smile then quickly devoured the rest of her carrot.

"My name is Isabelle. What's yours?"

Something slammed against the bars of their wagon. "No talking!"

Isabelle jerked away from the bars, anticipating another blow, though none came. She leaned back against the cold bars when the woman beside her pressed against her, the body heat welcome. She put her mouth to Isabelle's ear.

"Annette."

Simone Thibault Residence
Paris, Kingdom of France

"I'm not sure how long I'll be gone. Hopefully no more than a few days."

Mrs. Simone Thibault frowned at Thomas, the woman behind her desk as she usually was, even at this late hour, her bodyguard, Enzo, a massive tree trunk of a man, dutifully standing in the corner. "And what am I to do in the meantime? These accounts won't balance themselves. Do you expect me to do the math?" She flicked her wrist at the occupied corner of the room. "Enzo?"

The tree chuckled.

Thomas shook his head, trying to calm things. "No, of course not. I promise you I'll catch up when I return. I'll work all day and night, if necessary."

Thibault leaned back in her chair. "Oh, you'll do that, I guarantee you."

Thomas suppressed a sigh, his employer now sounding as if his departure would be permitted. He debated asking her about his neighbor's granddaughter, but decided it was best not to push his luck. "I'll send word if I'll be more than three days."

"You do that."

He headed for the door when she spoke again.

"And Thomas?"

He cringed, expecting the worst. "Yes, ma'am?"

"I hope you find your friend."

He wasn't sure what to say, this the kindest thing he had ever heard come from her mouth, and it left him frozen in place. If he expressed any sort of surprise, it might trigger her irrational temper, yet if he didn't acknowledge the kindness, it could do the same.

He glanced at the pile of muscles in the corner for guidance, but Enzo appeared just as shocked.

"Umm, thank you, ma'am." He took a chance, turning back toward her. "Ma'am, if I may, umm, I've been asked by a neighbor to inquire if you've heard anything of his granddaughter, a Miss Yvette Caron. She's been missing several days, and they fear the worst."

Thibault stared at him for a moment, her head slowly shaking. "What is it with these people? Don't they know who their granddaughters and daughters are? Don't these women talk to their elders?" She took a sip of her steaming tisane, then leaned back in her chair. "Yvette isn't missing, she's on a job."

Thomas' eyebrows shot up. "A job? For whom?"

"For me, of course."

He brightened with this new piece of information, at least confirming the girl was alive and not dead as he had feared. "Well, that's wonderful news! They'll be so relieved to hear that." He paused. "Umm, in anticipation of their questions, may I, umm, ask what the job is?"

Thibault laughed, tossing a smile at Enzo. "I think this week she's a nun who paddles misbehaving boys."

Thomas' eyes bulged. "Huh?"

Thibault shook her head, as if pitying a fool. "Oh, young one, you are so naïve. Do you not know what depravity lurks in this city we all call home? Do you not know the secret desires of the wicked? There are even depravities that I won't cater to, no matter the price offered. In this case, our beautiful Yvette was more than happy to put on a habit and spank a member of the aristocracy while swaddled for a few days. She'll earn a pretty piece of coin for the job, not have to give up access to her lady parts, and feed her family for a few weeks when she's finished."

Thomas had tuned out most of what was said, still staring at Thibault, his mouth agape. "Swaddled?"

Thibault grunted. "That's a tame one, my boy, a tame one. Those that lead us are a twisted lot. Many aren't just satisfied to bed a beautiful woman. They want something more. Much more. And quite often it has nothing to do with sex."

"Disgusting!"

Thibault shrugged. "To you, perhaps, though not necessarily to everyone else." She tapped her desk. "Though, as I said, there are lines even I won't cross, but others will."

Thomas shuddered, wondering what lines were worse than nuns

and swaddled noblemen. He drew a deep breath. "Umm, when will she be finished this, umm, job?"

"Tell her grandfather that she will be returning by morning."

Thomas sighed with relief, bowing his head. "Thank you, I will." He glanced at the door. "I, umm, better go. They'll be waiting for me."

Thibault flicked her wrist, dismissing him without a word. Enzo followed him down the stairs and out into the cold.

"I'll see you soon, Enzo."

"Take care of yourself, Master Thomas. If there's anything I can do for your lady friend, you let me know."

Thomas smiled. "I will." He bundled himself against the cold, then headed for home, feeling disturbingly comforted by his encounter. Thibault had wished Isabelle well, as had the lumbering pile of flesh and bone, Enzo. It was the kindliest encounter he could recall in that household, and it felt disturbingly like a family looking out for one another.

He shuddered.

If they were becoming his family, then he was truly lost.

Durant Residence
Paris, Kingdom of France

Marcus sat near the fire, enjoying the warmth, his body still not used to the harsh winters of his childhood. He could barely remember snow, yet knew he had already seen enough, and there were potentially months more of it ahead. He missed the desert heat, though if he had to think about it, escaping the cold was sometimes easier than the heat. Here, a warm fire was all one needed. In the Holy Land? The only remedy was night, or a swim.

Thomas entered, closing the door behind him and brushing the snow off his clothes before he began stripping the heavy garments off. "I'm sorry it took so long. I thought it best to let Mr. Caron know of what I found out about his granddaughter."

Marcus smiled. "Warm yourself by the fire and let us know what has happened." He pointed at the food and drink David had prepared in everyone's absence. "Eat. You must be starving."

"I am." Thomas sat cross-legged with the others, attacking the food.

"So, what did you find out?" asked Simon. "She lives?"

Thomas nodded. "Yes, apparently she is on a job for Mrs. Thibault."

"That's good news then. She is safe."

Thomas shrugged. "I suppose." He shuddered. "It disgusts me what she is doing."

Marcus frowned. "Is she defiling herself?"

Thomas grunted. "Perhaps her soul, but not her body."

Marcus' eyes narrowed. "I'm not sure I understand."

Thomas sighed. "I'm not sure I do, either." He shook his head. "It's too perverse to speak of."

Marcus agreed. "Then we won't. At least she is safe."

"Yes."

"And Mrs. Thibault. She didn't give you any trouble?"

Thomas shook his head as he polished off a piece of parsnip. "Not at all. If anything, she was quite understanding." He sighed. "*That* was disturbing as well."

Marcus' eyebrows rose slightly. "Why's that?"

Thomas shrugged. "I'm not used to her being nice, I guess."

"It is rather out of character."

A knock at the door had them all tensing, the hour very late for visitors. Thomas rose and opened the door, stepping back to let the father of the missing girl inside. He handed over something covered in a cloth after closing the door behind him.

"I'm sorry for the hour, but I figured since Master Thomas had just paid us a visit, you would still be awake." He removed the cloth, revealing a delicious looking fish pie. "My sister-in-law had baked an extra, and thought you might be hungry after your efforts on our behalf. We just wanted, as a family, to say thank you."

Marcus smiled, gesturing toward Thomas. "It was all Master Thomas' doing. He is the one to be thanked."

The man bowed his head to Thomas. "Thank you again." He hesitated. "I, umm, had a question, that I forgot to ask when you visited. Do you know what she is doing on this job?"

Thomas flushed, exchanging a quick glance with Marcus, and it was obvious the young man had no idea how to answer. From what he had volunteered moments ago, it sounded as if any honest answer could prove embarrassing for everyone involved. Marcus decided to save him. "I think that is something you must ask her. It was told to Thomas in the strictest of confidence, wasn't it?"

Thomas' eyes were wide, but he kept himself together enough to play along. "Umm, yes."

"And you don't dare violate that trust."

He shook his head vigorously. "No, absolutely not." He finally completed his recovery. "Mr. Caron, I can say that she went willingly, is apparently safe, and will return tomorrow. Should she not, let me know, and I will see what I can do."

Caron bowed again. "You are most kind, Thomas, most kind." He sighed. "We have been worried sick. When she returns, I shall tan her hide so she never has us worry like that again."

Marcus frowned. "Perhaps a stern word will be enough."

Caron flinched at Marcus' tone and bowed his head in deference. "Of course, m'Lord." He beat a hasty retreat and Thomas placed the pie at the center of the group, the assault from all sides taking place moments later.

Marcus took another bite from the end of his knife, savoring every chew, Caron's sister-in-law clearly a fine cook. He swallowed then took a swig of his drink. "Now, let's return to the business at hand. We need to find this priest."

Simon nodded. "Agreed, but how? There are probably hundreds of priests in Paris and the surrounding area. And we don't even know if he's from here."

"I can think of only one place to start."

Simon took another bite. "Where?"

"The Church itself."

His eyes narrowed. "Rome?"

Marcus shook his head. "No, here. The Cardinal. His people should know who is ordained to work here."

Thomas frowned. "Umm, I don't think he'll be very happy to see you."

Marcus regarded the young man. "Why?"

"Well, the Cardinal isn't exactly a fan of the Templars, if what I've heard is true."

Marcus' eyebrows rose slightly. "Really? I've been in the Holy Land for too long, apparently. I thought we were on good terms with the clergy."

Thomas shrugged. "Perhaps with the clergy there. Here? Things are very different in the Kingdom of France."

Marcus sighed. "Well, we'll find out tomorrow, won't we?"

Mortcerf, Kingdom of France

It had been a long, cold night, but after seeing the monks set up camp outside of the small village of Mortcerf, Jeremy had set up his own just out of sight. A small fire had allowed him to melt some snow and drink enough to fill his bladder, and as it should, the need to urinate had woken him before those he was tracking. And now, he watched as a sickening sight played out in the small town, another woman rounded up and shoved into the back of the wagon, as he imagined Isabelle had been the night before.

It was disgusting.

It was disturbing.

How a village could so quickly turn against one of its own was shocking. Terrifying. It threw into question everything he had imagined a family might be, what a family *should* be. He had never witnessed such betrayal within the Order, yet had seen it too often now that they had returned from the Holy Land and taken up as farmers and guardians.

When the question had been put to him on whether he wanted to stay with Sir Marcus, whose own choice had been forced upon him as it was his niece and nephew that needed caring for, he hadn't hesitated. Though the rest of them had a choice, there was but one correct one.

To stay.

He was loyal to Sir Marcus beyond anything. Though he loved the Order, and had one day hoped to make sergeant, those were merely selfish desires. At Sir Marcus' side was where he belonged.

Then the doubt had set in, and the shame at the questions he asked of himself. When Simon had disappeared, it had become a full-blown crisis of faith, for if Simon of all people could leave, a man who had known their master for over two decades, who had served him loyally that entire time as a brother and equal, then why should he, a mere squire, have to stay?

It was with relief he discovered David had the same questions, but when the truth surrounding Simon's disappearance had been revealed, his misconceptions challenged, and the depravity of the common man toward the unfamiliar and the different exposed, he realized his place was at his master's side, with his friends, and with the new family he was sworn to protect.

And he hadn't regretted a moment of his simple life on the farm since.

Yet today, here he was desperately tracking one of those he was supposed to have protected, and had failed to do so. Isabelle. Such a beautiful young woman, smitten with Marcus from the moment they had arrived, and now equally so with young Thomas, offered up willingly by the very people she had thought were her friends and family, to a priest who seemed mad, if his ravings were any indication.

As he crept closer to the village center, he could make out Isabelle cowering in the wagon with the others captured as a woman was led around by a chain, walking in some contorted manner, bent at the back, her feet and hands flat on the ground. If he couldn't hear her snarling, spitting ravings, he might have chalked it up to a carnival act, nothing more than a contortionist's sideshow.

But everything that went with it was terrifying, and his skin crawled at the sight.

Yet he had to push through it. And he had to provide some sort of comfort to Isabelle, to let her know that he was near, and that she wasn't alone.

The gathered crowd was distracted, as were the monks, all in a semi-circle, as if to hem in the possessed woman now paraded about by the priest. Nobody was watching the wagon, but if he were to run to it, he could easily be captured, and he couldn't risk it.

He was Isabelle's only hope.

As he pondered what to do, a thought occurred to him, and he smiled. If there was one thing he was known for, it was his skill as an archer. He drew an arrow and placed it on the bow, drawing back on the string. He took aim at the wagon, just below the bars holding the women inside, then loosed his arrow. It sliced through the air and embedded itself exactly where he had intended, in the wood at the base of the wagon, right below where Isabelle was cowering. She turned, apparently searching for the source of the sound, then reached through the bars and wrenched the arrow loose. She pulled it inside then clasped it against her chest.

He smiled.

Message received.

Outside Mortcerf, Kingdom of France

Isabelle's heart pounded as she gripped the arrow tight to her chest, and hopefully out of sight of the others. She wasn't sure why she had grabbed it, nor why she had been foolish enough to not only do so, but to keep it on her person.

It was madness.

Yet it was the only hint of comfort she had had since this ordeal began yesterday, for she knew what it represented. It was a message from either David or Jeremy. Both were experts with the bow, and both could have made that shot landing right below where she sat. And its message was clear.

You're not alone.

It brought tears to her eyes, and she struggled to maintain control as a sense of relief washed over her. She failed, her shoulders heaving, though just once.

But once was enough.

"What's wrong?" asked Annette.

Isabelle leaned nearer to the closest thing she had to a friend in this hell she found herself, and took a furtive glance at the others, to make certain they weren't watched. She rolled her shoulder, giving Annette a quick look at the arrow before tucking it back into the folds of her top.

"What is it?"

"It's a message from a friend."

Annette's eyes narrowed. "Message?"

Isabelle nodded, a slight smile on her face. "It means there's still hope."

"Hope?"

Isabelle flinched at the loudly spoken word from the woman sitting on the other side of Annette. Isabelle held a finger to her lips, but it was too late. Everyone was looking at them now, including the beast in the corner. It snarled and barked, pointing at her chest where the arrow wasn't entirely hidden, and her heart hammered as the ruckus continued to grow.

She quickly tossed the arrow between the bars and into the snow lining the road they were on, one of the monks calling for a halt to the procession. She stared out at where the arrow had landed, watching for any sign that one of the monks on horseback had spotted it, and was about to exhale with relief when the rear door opened, sending her into another panic.

"What's going on in here?" demanded one of the monks.

Isabelle curled into the smallest ball she could as Annette buried her head between Isabelle's back and the bars that held them, both trembling in unison.

The wretched creature spat out words that Isabelle couldn't understand, more of the demonic language she had heard referred to earlier, though this sounded different.

Latin?

Whatever it was, she couldn't understand, but the accusatory, bony finger that stabbed out at her she had no difficulty comprehending.

The evil woman was betraying her.

But why? Why would she do that? She was a prisoner just like the rest of them. Why would she help her captors?

And then she finally realized what was going on. Why she was a fool to be surprised.

This woman was evil incarnate, and of course an evil person would betray those who surrounded her, especially if they were innocent.

Isabelle glared at her, or it, as she had to accept it wasn't the woman at fault, but the demon that possessed her. And from the reaction of the others with her, she was convinced that the only one possessed among them was this creature that had betrayed her.

And she had done it not out of loyalty to the priest and his companions, but because it was her nature.

It was her nature to be cruel.

It was her nature to crush all hope.

It was her nature to be evil.

For she was not a she at all, but a demon in human form that Isabelle now knew could never be trusted.

And as Isabelle glared at the creature, she shuddered as the glare was returned.

And a sinister smile curled the edges of its lips.

Outside Mortcerf, Kingdom of France

"There might be a problem."

Father Mercier frowned at one of his men as they reported on the interruption. "What?"

"The Lost Cause told me that one of the girls had an arrow, and that she had said it was a message from someone."

Mercier sighed, his moisture-laden breath creating a mist in the ice cold air. The Lost Cause was what his men had taken to calling the poor soul whom he had repeatedly failed to save. She was the reason they had met, a wretched looking creature from the moment she had been brought to him, and she had proven a disappointment on numerous occasions. Each time he performed the exorcism on her, he appeared successful, then within days, sometimes hours, she would be returned by his men, the same foul-mouthed, despicable demon he had first met.

It was heartbreaking every time, though there was a small blessing he took from it. Her antics were so disturbing, that he had started using her as a demonstration of what the loved ones of the doubters could become, and one look at the Lost Cause's twisted, disjointed walk, was enough to convince anyone to willingly hand over their closest relation.

She had never failed.

Not once.

By showing those he encountered a woman so far gone, pushed so close to pure evil with no hope of ever being saved, he found that any doubts were always erased when she was put on display.

It was a sin, he knew, to use her like this in her current state, but her plight served a purpose, and thanks to her, many had been saved over the past couple of years since he'd been approached by the brothers, desperate to save the woman they now called the Lost Cause.

She had apparently been left at their abbey by a distraught family, and the monks had sought him out, knowing he had performed many an exorcism in his time.

But he had failed.

Miserably.

If anything, she had become worse, the demon possessing her establishing itself even more firmly.

Then the suggestion had been made, one he knew had been put on the lips of the monks by the Lord Himself. It was a suggestion that had saved his own soul.

To seek out, together, those that were afflicted, and to save them.

And they had been doing the Lord's work since, saving countless souls, the women returned to their grateful families by his faithful men.

And now, discontent was being sowed among those he was trying to save, and it had to be stopped.

"Which one?"

"The one we picked up in Crécy-la-Chapelle."

Mercier tensed. "The one with the Templar friends?"

The man nodded. "The very same."

He climbed down and made his way to the rear of the wagon, one of his men unlocking it and opening the door. He put on his sternest face, friendliness and sympathy useless when dealing with the beasts he had yet to save.

"I understand one of you is causing problems."

Unsurprisingly, no one said anything, instead all of them pushing away from him slightly, likely terrified of the crucifix around his neck.

"Which one of you was it?"

He already knew the answer, but the Lost Cause confirmed it with a quick glance of betrayal toward the beautiful creature they had collected in Crécy-la-Chapelle, as his man had said.

The one with two troublesome friends.

He didn't acknowledge the silent message, not wanting to give any sort of twisted pleasure or satisfaction to the demon that possessed the Lost Cause. Instead, he stared at each of them, the evil in their eyes deadening his soul slightly, a necessary risk if he were to perform the sometimes violent ritual on these women when they finally arrived at his church.

He had to remember that despite their terrifying visages, these were women, innocent women, like his mother, trapped inside, their bodies taken over by Satan's servants.

He alone could see not only their true selves, but the evil that lurked within, a gift from the Lord Himself, he was certain. And each of the women that stared back at him showed both terror at what had become of them, and rage at what was to be done to them.

For if he succeeded, all that would be left would be the young women, innocent, pure, and beautiful. Women who could return to their lives and raise their children to a ripe old age, when they would then be taken from this Earth at the proper time, to join the Lord in His dominion.

His eyes came to rest on the one in question, on the one called Isabelle, if he recalled correctly, and he smiled at the evil on display, knowing it would drive the creature mad, but would also show his strength and determination to the possessed girl within.

"Fear not, my child, for soon you will be freed of this evil, and returned to those who love you." He stepped back and the door was slammed shut then locked. He walked several paces away, out of earshot of the possessed, one of his men at his side. "I think our Templar squires have returned."

"Agreed. What should we do?"

Mercier thought for a moment, staring back at the road they were traveling. "At least one of them is obviously following us."

"We can't have that."

"No, we can't." He sighed, his heart heavy with what he had to do. It wasn't the fault of these Templars. They had been corrupted by the evil that lay within young Isabelle, her beauty causing them to do foolish things they wouldn't normally do. If they hadn't been so deceived, they would have accepted his word that she was an occupied soul, and left him to do his work.

But instead, they continued to interfere, and put everything he had worked for at risk.

And for that, there was only one response.

"Leave six men behind to intercept them."

"Six? Are you sure?"

"Yes. This must be stopped immediately." He frowned, gripping his crucifix tight. "I think we'll cut our trip short and head back to the church. I don't want to risk any interference from these Templars. It's clear that if they are out to save this Isabelle, then they too are either possessed, or they serve Satan willingly. Either way, should your men encounter them, kill them so they can't interfere with God's work."

His man bowed. "It shall be done, Father."

Cardinal Nicolas' Office, Notre-Dame de Paris
Paris, Kingdom of France

Marcus was slightly taken aback at the vehement response to their simple query. Cardinal Nicolas l'Aide had leaped from his seat the moment the words had come from Sir Marcus' mouth, mentioning a priest traveling with a group of armed monks, performing exorcisms.

"The very notion that a member of the clergy would perform unsanctioned exorcisms is offensive and dangerous!" cried the man, his face almost as crimson as his robes. "For you to even suggest such a thing on sacred ground is an affront to not only me, but His Holiness and the Church itself!"

Marcus bowed deeply, as did Sir Denys who had accompanied him to make their granting of an audience at least a possibility. Marcus had a feeling the man was now regretting the offer to assist. "I meant no disrespect, Your Eminence. Clearly, our information is incorrect. This man must not be a priest, and those with him must not be monks."

Denys scrambled to assist. "We are obviously dealing with imposters."

Cardinal Nicolas appeared unwavering in his anger. "This is what happens when rumor and innuendo are allowed to be spoken freely in our society." He jabbed a finger at Denys. "You, I expected better of. You're nobility! You know how deeply the Church loves its children, all its children in this great kingdom." He glared at Marcus. "But you, a Templar, I've come to expect such treachery by those in your order. You have been corrupted by unchecked power and the untold wealth you wield." His hands balled into fists as he leaned forward on his desk. "Mark my words, Templar, one of these days, your order will be called to answer for your crimes. Don't be adding to them by spreading these lies that the Church is abducting innocent women from the surrounds of Paris." He pushed off the desk, folding his arms. "If I hear even a mention of this again, I'll see you hanged for blasphemy."

Marcus bowed again. "I think it is best we withdraw, Your Eminence. I'm sorry to have offended you."

He headed for the door, Denys on his heels, saying nothing more. The Cardinal's threats didn't bother him, instead, they simply made him curious. Why would the man react so violently to a simple query? Shouldn't he be concerned that there might be someone out there whose actions might besmirch the Church? Shouldn't he demand answers, rather than hurl threats?

None of it made sense.

As they left the building, Simon and David waiting for them outside with the horses, Marcus exchanged a glance with Denys, who seemed as surprised as he was.

"Well?" asked Simon as he handed the reins over to Marcus. "What did you find out?"

Marcus shook his head. "Not here."

They left the grounds where the Cardinal's powers were absolute, and returned to Denys' estate with nothing else said. Secure within the walls of the aristocrat, Marcus finally exploded.

"What was that all about?"

Denys shook his head. "Evidently, the Cardinal has a dislike for your order."

Simon growled. "Will someone please tell us what is going on?"

Marcus dropped into a chair, the others doing the same. "We were granted an audience with little problem, thanks to Sir Denys, however, the moment I related what had happened to Isabelle, and to Lord Allard's daughter, he became irate."

Denys grunted. "Enraged! I've never seen a member of the clergy become so angry. It was as if we had personally accused him of the crime."

Marcus agreed. "He did indeed become irrational. He even admonished Sir Denys for his involvement in our inquiries."

"And threatened your order with a reckoning." Denys shook his head. "It was most disturbing."

David's eyes were wide with disbelief. "He threatened the Order?"

Marcus nodded. "Yes. It was quite the spectacle. Very undignified."

Simon growled. "This must be reported."

Marcus agreed. "And it will be, the next time we are at the Fortress."

David sighed. "Well, it would appear that young Thomas was right about the Cardinal's dislike of Templars."

Marcus frowned. "I had thought he was perhaps overreacting to something heard and misunderstood, but after this morning's display, I fear he is absolutely right." He shook his head. "And what disturbs me more is that if someone like him knows this, then much of Paris must know. And for the head of the Church in Paris to openly revile the Order, an order sanctioned by His Holiness himself, is rather remarkable."

Denys cleared his throat. "I'm afraid it *is* rather well known among the Court, though I wasn't aware it had made its way to the common folk. But for him to display such open hostility in a manner such as this, something that should concern the Church, is rather remarkable." He crossed his arms. "The question now is what do we do? Without the help of the Church, how do we find this priest?"

Simon grunted. "There can't be too many going about performing exorcisms, can there?"

Marcus shrugged. "It would be a rather specialized thing, I would think, though I've never seen one performed."

Simon shook his head. "Nor I."

"Nor I as well," said Denys.

David shrugged. "Since I spend most of my days with you two, it's safe to say I've never seen one either, though to be honest, I don't know if I'd recognize one if I saw it."

Marcus chuckled at the comment. "If we're being honest, I too wouldn't know what to look for."

Denys nodded. "There is someone I know, someone I think I can trust, that might be able to help us."

"Who?"

"The priest at my church, at the palace. I've known him for years, and if anyone would know, it would be him."

"And you're sure he can be trusted."

"Yes, I believe so."

Marcus thought for a moment, scratching at an imagined itch in his beard, as he thought of the threat implied by the Cardinal. He shook his head. "No, we can't risk word getting back to the Cardinal that we're still pursuing the matter."

"Then what would you have us do?" asked Denys.

"I think we need to change our tactics."

Simon's eyes narrowed. "What do you mean?"

"I think, perhaps, a little theater might serve us better."

Denys leaned back in his chair. "What the Devil are you talking about?"

Marcus smiled. "The Devil indeed."

Outside Mortcerf, Kingdom of France

Jeremy watched from his hidden position as the priest climbed back onto the wagon and the procession got underway again, the entourage disappearing into the forest and out of sight.

And it had him concerned.

Something had happened that had made them stop, something unusual, for the rear of the wagon had been opened and a conversation had. This was something he had never observed before, and he feared it might be because of him.

Had the arrow been discovered? He had been happy to provide some hope to Isabelle, but she should have immediately disposed of the arrow, rather than keep it with her. If it had been discovered, then they would know someone was following them.

Yet if they knew, they were giving no indication that they did. The entire group had left together. None had been left behind to intercept him, so perhaps something else had happened that had caused the unusual stoppage.

Whatever it was, it was over now, and the wagon was out of sight. He returned to his horse and mounted her, urging her forward at an easy gait, as there was no point in risking catching up to Isabelle's captors, and the large group was leaving a distinct impression on the fresh snow that was easy to follow.

As he entered the dense forest, the sunlight pushing through the overcast sky dimmed, and he turned to his other senses to keep him alert, though the sounds of these forests were unfamiliar. In the Holy Land, he knew instantly every sound he heard, man, beast, or nature, but here, here everything was new, everything was unfamiliar.

And it made him uneasy.

He frowned, spotting what appeared to be at least one horse splitting off from the group and heading into the trees. There could be any number of reasons, but too many of them weren't good, and Jeremy slowed up, listening intently as he peered into the darkened forest, the canopy overhead thick from the ancient trees.

Anybody could be hiding in there, and it made him nervous. He was pursuing a dozen armed men on horseback, and they could spare a handful to check for pursuers.

And if they had indeed found the arrow, they would know there was one to look for.

He readied his bow, scanning the area for any sign, as he tried to remember if he had seen any bows among the monks. He was fairly certain he hadn't, which provided him with a small amount of comfort.

Any attack would have to be on horseback, by sword.

It meant he might have time to take out whoever attacked at a distance, and at least flee should it become necessary.

His horse's right ear swiveled and he cursed at what was to come. Pounding hooves charged toward him from ahead, and he turned his ride, readying it for a quick getaway as he drew his bow.

Something moved to his left.

A monk, his dark robes having obscured him, rushed from behind a tree, his sword already swinging at Jeremy's exposed side. Jeremy twisted around to take aim at the unexpected attacker, but it was too late. The blade slammed into his side and he gasped as several ribs cracked under his chainmail. He fell to the side and out of the saddle as the riders that had distracted him came into sight. He reached up with his bow, still gripped in his hand, and smacked the hindquarters of his horse, sending her into a gallop as he struggled to regain his seat, but it was no use, his injured side blinding him with pain.

He fell to the ground, then to his horror, he continued to be dragged by the panicking animal, his foot caught in the stirrup. He struggled to free himself, part of him wondering if that were wise, as it would leave him in the hands of the monks.

But his debate wasn't to last long, as his head hit something hard, his world going dark, as his horse continued to drag him perhaps to safety.

Perhaps to death.

Sainte-Chapelle, Palais de la Cité
Paris, Kingdom of France

"Father, I have a friend who is in trouble."

Denys knelt in the confessional of his church, a place he had spent a lot of time in over the past several months with so many sins to confess. It had been overwhelming, and certainly humiliating. The punishments handed out by his priest, a man he had known for years, were harsh, but were necessary if his soul was to be saved.

And with each day of prayer, with each visit, he had felt better about himself, despite having strayed from the path he was certain the Lord had intended for him.

Yet none of that mattered today, for today he was here to lie to a priest, to *his* priest, and it was tearing him up inside.

And it had him wondering how the confession to the sin he was now committing would go over next week.

Perhaps I should confess elsewhere.

"What sort of trouble, my son."

"It's his daughter. He thinks she's possessed by some sort of demon."

There was no response on the other side of the confessional, and Denys wondered if Marcus' plan was indeed as foolish and dangerous as Denys had thought.

"That is most troubling. What evidence of possession is there?"

Fortunately, his past had made him an accomplished liar, and he knew that the fewer the details, the more chance there was that the lie would succeed. "You have to understand, Father, that my friend is most distressed by this, and, of course, embarrassed, so he has given me few details. Apparently, she must be restrained at all times, spits and snarls and screams the most revolting of obscenities, things no young woman should ever say, let alone have ever heard in order to repeat them."

"Does she speak in the Devil's tongue?"

He sounds anxious.

It would appear the lie was working, though he had to be careful. He had no idea what the Devil's tongue was, but decided an answer to the affirmative was in order. "If you mean in a language none of those surrounding her have ever heard, then I believe yes."

"You must have your friend bring his daughter here at once."

Denys shook his head. "I'm afraid that's not possible. He is too public a figure. Is there someone else, someone from outside this church, who could perform the ritual, the exorcism, I believe you call it?"

124

"It is an incredibly dangerous, demanding thing, and few priests willingly take on the task. Even I have only performed one, and it was many years ago when I was much younger." There was a pause. "I will give you a list of names and their churches. I'm certain you will find one that can perform the exorcism with the level of discretion that your friend requires."

Denys suppressed a smile. "Thank you, Father. My friend will be most generous in his appreciation, I am certain."

Outside Mortcerf, Kingdom of France

"He won't be returning."

Isabelle kept her eyes closed as she pretended to sleep, having woken only moments before to the sounds of hooves pounding as the monks left behind returned. Her heart hammered as she listened for any word on the fate of her friends, then it broke with those overheard words.

"There was just one?" asked Father Mercier.

"Yes."

Mercier grunted. "Then that means the other might have gone for help."

"Perhaps, but he'll have no way of finding us, now that his friend is out of the picture."

"Dead?"

Isabelle held her breath.

"He managed to get away, but not before I sliced open his side. He'll be dead in short order."

"I will pray for his soul, as you all should. It wasn't his fault that he was seduced by the succubus we now carry. Any of us could have succumbed to her wiles if put in his position of constant contact. *This* is exactly why we do what we do, so that others like that poor Templar squire don't lose their lives in unknowing service to the Devil." Mercier paused as tears flowed freely down Isabelle's cheeks. "Did you lose any men?"

"None. We were fortunate he was alone. Our ambush likely would not have been successful if his partner had been with him."

"Indeed." The wagon moved again with a flick of the reins. "Let's make all haste for the church. With his friend still out there, I have concerns. Send a messenger to Saint-Julien and let the others know to prepare for our arrival tomorrow."

"Yes, Father."

Isabelle finally gasped out her held breath, her shoulders letting go with a furious series of shakes as she imagined which one of her friends was now dead, and hating herself for hoping it was David over Jeremy, for it was David who had held Jeremy back.

He did what he had to.

If David and Jeremy had done anything that first night, they would have both died right then. But with one of them still out there, it meant Sir Marcus knew, and if anyone could save her, could save them all, it was him.

She said a silent prayer for both David and Jeremy, wiping away her tears, and with no point in faking sleep anymore, she finally opened her eyes.

And immediately spotted the evil one staring at her, a smile on her face, a smile that held none of the warmth it should.

Saint-Étienne Church
Paris, Kingdom of France

Marcus sighed as the last possibility was stricken from their list. Sir Denys had been provided with a list of priests that might be willing to perform an exorcism on his fake friend's daughter, and none had proven to be the one they were after. All had been in Paris for weeks, if not longer, and even if they were lying, the very fact they were in the city now would have meant that Jeremy would also be here, and would have gotten word to them already.

"My being in Paris for the past several years bothers you?"

Marcus shook his head at Father Brodeur. "No, Father, it doesn't. It's something else that vexes me."

Brodeur regarded him for a moment, his forefinger tapping on his chin. "I get the distinct impression, my son, that you were not looking for someone to perform an exorcism, but that you are in fact looking for a *specific* exorcist. Am I right?"

Marcus frowned at the question, but decided he was finished with lying to priests, at least for today. "If I'm to be honest with you, Father, I am indeed looking for someone specific."

Brodeur chuckled, wagging a finger at him. "You should always be honest with a member of the clergy, my son. Tell me the truth, and perhaps I can help you."

Marcus smiled. "You're right, of course, Father, and I am ashamed at the subterfuge."

"When we are done, you will confess your sins. Before that, tell me what it is you truly seek."

Marcus felt slightly better at the understanding shown, and took a deep breath. "I'm looking for a man whom I believe is a priest, who is accompanied by a group of monks armed with swords, who are taking beautiful women across the countryside, claiming they are possessed."

Brodeur appeared taken aback by the description, and he paled slightly. He looked for the nearest chair then unceremoniously dropped into it. "I, umm, believe I may know who you are talking about, but I can assure you he is no member of the clergy."

Marcus' heart hammered at the possibility of progress as he took a seat across from the man. "Who? Who is he?"

"If it's who I think it is, his name is Hugo Mercier. He attended the University while I was teaching there a few years ago, but after consulting with the Cardinal, we agreed he wasn't a good fit."

Marcus' eyes narrowed at the mention of the Cardinal who had threatened the Order earlier that morning. "Why wasn't he a good fit?"

"He was obsessed with demonic possessions. He believed that all beautiful women were the work of the Devil, and that their souls must be cleansed. When I told him he was being expelled, he swore he'd perform his work with or without the blessing of the church."

"When was this?"

"Two, perhaps three years ago."

"And you think it might be him?"

"Shortly after he left the University, I heard rumors of an exorcist traveling with a group of monks, but it was only a rumor. I really thought nothing of it, as I couldn't believe any monk, let alone a group of them, would agree to follow an unordained priest."

Marcus pursed his lips. "This Father Mercier. Is there any way we might find him?"

Brodeur shook his head. "Not that I know of. Certainly not through the Church."

Marcus' eyebrows shot up. "My squire said that this priest made mention of taking our friend to *his* church. Is it possible he could be actually operating out of one?"

Brodeur's eyes widened and he shook his head vehemently. "Absolutely not!"

Marcus chewed his cheek as he thought. "What about an abandoned church? Is that a possibility?"

Brodeur's head slowly bobbed, a finger tapping his left earlobe. "If he is indeed working out of a church, it would have to be an abandoned one, you're right. Unfortunately, there are many of those in the area."

"It would have to be near Paris, perhaps even inside Paris."

"Again, there could be many, though there are few abandoned churches actually inside the city." He sighed. "I'm afraid I'm the wrong one to ask. The Cardinal's people would know, however."

Marcus frowned. "The Cardinal doesn't appear very interested in helping us, unfortunately."

Brodeur nodded. "Yes, I'm afraid his opinion of the Templars is not very good." He snapped his fingers, a smile spreading. "But I have a friend who might be willing to help you. He's an archivist for the Church, and might be able to give you the information you're looking for."

Marcus smiled. "I would be eternally grateful."

Brodeur rose. "Good. Now, how about that confession? I have a feeling you have much to unburden yourself of."

Marcus tensed, wondering if he'd have any time for the penance he was about to receive after lying to priests all day.

Unknown Location, Kingdom of France

"What's happened to you, young one?"

Jeremy groaned, forcing his eyes open, then snapping them shut as his head pounded in pain, only to be overwhelmed by the agony of his left side. Somebody slapped his cheek and he opened his eyes once more to find an old woman, a hag if there ever was one, leaning over him, along with the snout of his horse.

She pulled up his tunic, revealing his chainmail underneath. "Looks like you took quite the hit, young one. You got lucky. Your armor protected you." She rapped on his ribs and he winced, gasping for breath. "I'd say you broke a few of these, wouldn't you?"

"It doesn't feel lucky." He struggled to a seated position, searing pain his constant companion with every move, before gasping out a reply. "I've definitely broken some ribs."

The old woman stood straight. "Better some broken ribs than being cleaved like the deliverer of that blow intended."

Jeremy grunted. "True." He pushed to his feet then steadied himself against his horse as he caught his breath. He glanced up at the sky, trying to determine how long he had been unconscious, then cried out as the old woman did something to his back. "What the Devil?"

"Oh, I don't think this is the work of the Devil." She yanked at something and he gasped, his enraged ribs punishing him almost to the point of collapse. She presented him with a short stick, one end of it bloodied. "I'd say it was the work of Mother Nature, wouldn't you?"

He frowned, gingerly rotating his shoulder.

"Don't worry, it wasn't in deep. You'll live, should you desire it."

His eyes narrowed. "Should?"

"You were attacked by monks. Surely there must be something wrong with you if men of the Church want you dead."

He grunted. "I'm not so certain they serve the same church I do."

The old woman nodded. "Armed monks. Not something you see every day." She slapped the Templar cross on his tunic, causing him to cry out from the assault on his ribs. "Then again, you're some sort of warrior monk, aren't you?"

He frowned. "Of sorts." He stared up at the sky again, detecting a dull glow behind the clouds. It had clearly been hours since he was knocked out, leaving the wagon with Isabelle long gone. He was in too much pain for a hard ride to catch up, and where they might have gone was anyone's guess.

He had failed.

He turned to the old lady. "You wouldn't happen to know where they went?"

She laughed and pointed down the road. "That way."

He chuckled at the only choice there was. "I suppose it was a stupid question."

She agreed. "Yes, it was. Now, I must be off. It will be snow tonight, I think. You'd best find shelter soon."

"I will." Jeremy mounted his horse, the effort agonizing and exhausting. He looked down at the woman. "Can I give you a ride somewhere?"

She shook her head, pointing into the nearby woods. "I live just there. I only came out to see what had become of you." She flicked a hand at him. "Now go. Your commandry isn't far from here. Only a couple of hours from here in your state."

Jeremy suddenly had hope. "Which one?"

"Coulommiers."

He smiled, recognizing it. "I know it! I guess I lost track of where I was." He bowed his head. "Thank you, madam, for your assistance. I bid you a good day."

She batted a hand at him, striking out from the road and toward the woods, retracing a path carved in the snow by her venture outside. He watched her disappear into the trees, then urged his horse on at as fast a pace as he could stand, mentally composing the message he would be sending Sir Marcus, recounting his failure, while praying for the safety of poor Isabelle.

Archives, Notre-Dame de Paris
Paris, Kingdom of France

Marcus frowned as the archivist Father Brodeur had referred them to continued to mark churches within two days' ride of Paris that his records indicated were abandoned. There were dozens, and this was looking more and more like a fool's errand.

Serge Courtier flipped shut the bound pages he had been referring to before pushing the completed map toward his guests. "That is as best as I can do for you, I'm afraid."

Denys picked up the map, shaking his head. "You mean there could be more?"

Courtier nodded. "Yes, though if they aren't on my list, they're so old, they're most likely in a state of repair that would leave them little more than a pile of stones."

"And these ones?" asked Marcus. "They are useable?"

Courtier shrugged. "According to our latest survey, these could be reoccupied with some work."

Denys looked up from the map. "And when was this survey?"

Courtier turned away for a moment. "Fifteen years ago."

Denys' jaw dropped. "Then this could be useless!"

Courtier became defensive, crossing his arms. "I've done my best! I can only work with the information at hand!"

Marcus patted Denys on the shoulder, delivering as calming a smile as he could to the rotund man who had done them a favor against the Cardinal's wishes. "I have no doubt you've done your best, and it is truly appreciated."

Courtier grunted. "Your friend has an odd way of showing it."

Marcus swatted Denys on the shoulder, and the man gave him a look before bowing his head. "I'm sorry for my outburst. It has been a trying couple of days, and we are desperate to find these missing women."

Courtier squirmed in his chair for a moment, then beamed a smile back at them. "Oh, all right, apology accepted. I guess we're all a little testy now that it's winter." He pointed at the map. "The locals have a habit of stealing the stones over time, especially the farther out you go. I recommend sticking closer to the city. People are less likely to steal from the site of a church when there are eyes around to see their sin."

Marcus nodded. "Excellent advice, thank you." He tapped the map to the east of the city. "We'll start in the east, since we know that's where he was last seen. Hopefully, we'll get lucky." He rolled up the map and bowed to Courtier. "Thank you once again for your assistance. I'll be sure to let Lord Allard know should we be successful."

Courtier waved both hands in front of him, shaking his head vigorously. "No! I don't want my name involved at all. I did this as a favor to Father Brodeur. If the Cardinal were to find out I helped Templars, it would be my head."

Marcus frowned. "He really doesn't like our order, does he? Any idea why?"

Courtier shrugged. "It's not my business to know, but I would give him a wide berth if I were you."

Marcus smiled. "Sage advice, I'm sure."

They left Courtier's post in the basement of the cathedral and collected their horses from David. "There are four of us. I suggest we split up the list to save time." He tore the map in four strips from east to west, handing one segment each to Simon, Denys, and David. "We'll meet at Thomas' at nightfall. Remember, observe and report. If you find anything, don't act, just return. One person against a dozen monks will be no match."

Simon grunted. "For you, perhaps."

Marcus smiled, but jabbed his sergeant in the chest. "Observe and report."

Simon sighed. "Fine, fine, I'll report what I find so you can return and save the day."

Marcus grinned. "Now you're getting it!"

Templar Commandry

Coulommiers, Kingdom of France

"What do you intend to do?"

Jeremy drew as deep a breath as he could, testing the limits of the bandages the nuns were binding him with as Sir Raimond de Comps stood several paces away, his arms folded across his chest, while Jeremy brought him up to speed on what had happened. "I'm afraid there's not much I can do beyond joining Sir Marcus in Paris, I suppose. I think there's little hope of finding Isabelle now."

Sir Raimond nodded. "There's a storm brewing, so you'll be stuck here until at least morning."

Jeremy shook his head. "No, I can't wait. She's my responsibility, and I've already failed her once."

Raimond stepped closer. "Son, your death will do little to help her."

Jeremy winced at a slightly rough tug from one of the nuns, giving him the distinct impression that they agreed with their master, and that his leaving before a storm would render their treatment of his wounds moot. "I know, but besides David, I'm the only one who has seen this priest. If he's to be found, my eyes might be key."

Raimond shook his head slowly. "You're a fool, but brave, I'll give you that. I'll make sure you're provisioned for such a journey, but with those ribs, I fear you won't make it far."

Jeremy nodded. "I appreciate your concern, but I have to try."

Outskirts of Paris, Kingdom of France

David held his hand up to shield his eyes, the snow coming down hard now, the wind whipping it into a blinding frenzy. He had checked half the churches on his portion of the map, and had come up empty at each one. As he urged his poor steed forward, he spotted the next church ahead, the dark, imposing stone standing out against the white of the snow, if only faintly.

He drew a quick breath in excitement as he caught a hint of something, an orange glow that could only be fire.

Someone was there.

He hunkered down, pushing forward, his heart hammering from the fear gripping him from the first winter storm of his adult life experienced outside of the safety of the farm, and from the unknown that lay ahead. His orders were to return and report what he found, and Marcus had specifically said not to take action. But he had to make sure it wasn't simply vagrants taking shelter from the storm.

He crossed a small stone bridge, the church just ahead, the humble structure in apparent good shape from what he could see from this angle. The glow of torches or fires inside highlighted the cracks in the shutters covering the windows, and suggested the walls and roof were intact.

Would an abandoned church still have shutters?

He wouldn't think so. If the other churches he had seen earlier were any indication, the edifices were stripped bare, even the stones taken like the archivist had apparently said. It made sense. He would assume the Church would take anything of value, then the locals would take anything left, and quarried stone was valuable.

Though this place appeared intact, or at least mostly so. He could now see that the spire that once held the cross had partially collapsed, and surprisingly, there wasn't a new one in place. Wouldn't a priest have made that one of his first priorities? Though perhaps, if this priest was who Father Brodeur thought he might be, he wasn't a priest at all.

But he had certainly acted like one, at least in the brief encounter he and Jeremy had had with him.

I hope Jeremy is okay.

The storm, he was certain, would force the priest to seek shelter, and he would have the benefit of not being forced to be secretive. Jeremy would likely be forced to shelter outside, or risk losing the wagon should they depart while he slept.

I hope the fool doesn't get too close.

He shivered against the cold and the thought of what might happen to his friend, his best friend, should he encounter the armed monks.

His heart hammered as he realized how close he now was to the church.

Follow your own advice, idiot.

He had seen enough to know that someone was here. They could return in the morning and investigate in numbers should the others have not found what they were seeking.

He tugged on the reins and turned his horse around, then gasped as he found the bridge blocked by half a dozen men.

Men in dark robes, with swords drawn.

Outskirts of Paris, Kingdom of France

Marcus stared up at the sky, the sun getting low, the clouds thick as the flurries falling most of the afternoon turned to heavy flakes, quickly adding to the snow already on the ground. So far, his search had proven fruitless, and the light was quickly fading. He still had several churches left on his list, but the weather was turning quickly, and with the reduced visibility, it was simply too dangerous to risk running into the very people he was seeking.

He turned back toward the city, less than half an hour's ride from his current position, and urged his horse forward, squinting into the unfamiliar snow. Having spent decades in the Holy Land, snow was not something he was used to, nor was the bitter cold. The desert could be frigid at night, but this was an entirely different level of cold. He was sure he'd get used to it eventually, all the locals who had lived here their entire lives seemingly fine with the weather, but today his bones were rattling and his teeth were chattering.

And his toes and fingertips were tingling as if the circulation to them had been cut off.

That can't be good.

He urged his horse on a little harder, the poor beast probably feeling the cold as acutely as he was. A good pace would hopefully keep her warm, and the stables at the end of their journey would give her time to recover.

The time to the outskirts of the city passed quickly, the adrenaline fueling him helping keep him alert. As soon as the road leading to Paris turned into a street lined with buildings, the wind cut down considerably and the visibility improved dramatically, along with his mood and that of his horse. The only light now was the gentle glow of fires and lanterns inside the buildings he passed, and it did little to help him as he picked his way through the still unfamiliar city.

Fortunately, he had an excellent sense of direction, and soon found himself in the right neighborhood, with enough familiar landmarks to lead him to Thomas' humble home. He hitched his horse then pushed open the door, a roaring fire with no expense spared casting a welcome glow and warmth across the room. He smiled at Simon and Thomas, sitting as close to the fire as they could safely manage, both attacking another fish pie.

His eyes narrowed. "Where's David?"

Simon shrugged. "Not back yet. Probably the storm."

Marcus frowned as he stripped out of his gear. "It's bad out there, so you might be right. And Sir Denys?"

"He was here earlier," replied Thomas as he rose to help Marcus, waving Simon off. "He found nothing. He's returned home, and said he will be pleased to continue the search tomorrow."

"Good. And did you two find anything?"

Simon shook his head. "Nothing, just abandoned churches with no evidence they had been used by anyone but vagrants for years."

Thomas frowned. "I was equally unsuccessful, I'm afraid."

Marcus, freed of his trappings, sat by the fire, Thomas handing him a spoon before resuming his previous position.

Simon swallowed a bite. "Did you find anything?"

Marcus took a bite, his stomach rumbling. "Nothing." He shivered, then remembered his horse was still outside, unaccustomed to one of his squires not being around to tend to it. "I must see to my horse."

Thomas held out a hand then jumped to his feet. "No, I'll do it. You stay by the fire, you look frozen."

Marcus smiled, no fight left in him. He took another bite of the pie. "Where'd this come from?"

"Yvette's family again," replied Thomas as he dressed for the cold. "Apparently, she returned earlier today, and the family was grateful."

Marcus took another bite. "Hopefully they stay grateful. This is delicious."

Thomas grinned. "Let's hope." He disappeared out the door, a chill rushing through the home before the door closed and the fire reasserted its dominance.

"So, what did you think of the cold?"

Simon grunted. "Beyond ridiculous. It's almost enough to make me think an eternity in Hades might be preferable to another winter of this."

Marcus chuckled. "Careful what you wish for." He frowned as he chewed, his thoughts returning to their situation. "I'm concerned about David and Jeremy. I don't like them both being out there alone."

Simon stuck his spoon in "his" side of the pie, leaving it there. "I'm not worried about David. He'll show up soon enough, though he might be a block of ice." He held out his hands. "Did you feel your fingers and toes? What was that about?"

Marcus nodded, finally noticing the feeling returning to his extremities in a slightly painful way. "I did. Very strange. Let's ask Thomas about it when he returns." He took another bite. "But you're right. I don't think David is the one to worry about, it's young Jeremy."

Simon grunted. "Not so young anymore."

"True, though I still find myself picturing him as the boy he was when he first began to serve me."

"He was an ugly runt, if I recall."

Marcus laughed. "And so awkward. But he grew out of it. He's turned into a fine man, and an excellent squire."

"He should be a sergeant by now. So should David."

Marcus frowned. "They both made their choice years ago to remain as they are."

"True, but was it the right choice?"

Marcus regarded his friend. "For selfish reasons, I say yes. I'd hate to have to train new squires at my age."

Simon laughed. "Good point. And I do like the lads. Much more tolerable than some of the others I've encountered over the years."

Thomas returned, closing the door behind him and shaking from his clothes the snow that had accumulated in the short time he had been gone. "It's pretty bad out there. If David doesn't get back soon, he might have to seek shelter elsewhere."

Marcus frowned. "He's equipped if he has to, but let's hope it doesn't come to that. His search area was mostly on the outskirts. If he makes his way into the city, the visibility improves."

The entire house shook from a gust of wind, as if God were begging to differ.

"What should we do?" asked Simon.

"There's nothing we can do. We'll wait until morning before we go looking for him. Hopefully, the storm will have broken by then, and we know where his assigned search area was, so we'll just follow his planned route."

"He has the map. How are we going to manage that?"

Marcus tapped his temple. "It's all up here."

Simon growled. "That memory of yours scares me sometimes."

Marcus shrugged. "I consider it a gift from God."

"I wish I had that gift."

Marcus smiled. "He obviously likes me better."

Two hours outside Coulommiers, Kingdom of France

You're an idiot.

Jeremy wasn't sure how many times he had called himself that, or variations thereof, but it was more than he could count. The storm was setting in, and he had made little progress, his ribs making it difficult to set a good pace, his breathing shallow from the tight bandages, and the road increasingly covered in heavy snow.

His horse could only do so much.

And so could he.

He had to find shelter. There was no denying that now, yet he refused to go backward. He had left the last town at least an hour ago, and another had to be along the road soon, but he was rapidly getting weaker, and needed what strength he had left to set up camp and get a fire started, otherwise he'd die for sure.

The latest gust of wind suddenly stopped, everything settling for a brief moment, and Jeremy smiled at what was revealed by the good Lord above.

A barn.

Or at least some of one.

He turned off the road, the remains of a burnt out house nearby indicating the property was abandoned, but a barn in still reasonable shape sat nearby. He dismounted and opened the door, smiling at the sight. Four walls—or three and a half—most of a roof, and some discarded hay.

He led the horse inside then closed the door, the bite of the wind instantly reduced. He unpacked his mount, leading her to the hay, then set to starting a fire with the supplies provided at the commandry. Within minutes, he had a small fire going, then kept feeding it with scraps of wood lying about, before stoking it as best he could for the night. He thawed some snow for both him and the horse, and ate as many of his provisions as he could manage before finally giving in to the pain and cold, lying as close to the fire as he could, praying the Lord would deliver him from his own stupidity.

En route to Paris, Kingdom of France

Isabelle shivered against the cold, huddled with the others as the storm made its presence known, even the evil one joining into the mound of human flesh sharing their body heat. Their captors were all comfortable in tents surrounding the wagon, the only protection given to the women were cloth sides lowered to cut down the wind.

It was a small blessing.

They had been fed a hot meal, soup and bread, the first solid meal since she had been captured, and she was certain that was just to help keep them alive through the night.

As she squeezed her eyes tight, pressed up against Annette, another girl pressed against her back, she prayed for God to deliver her from this Hell she found herself in, and once again apologized for what she had said about Garnier.

Nonsense!

An ember of anger flared in her chest as she thought about what was happening to her, and the minor transgression of yesterday. What she had done was wrong, but this punishment was far beyond anything that might be considered reasonable.

And it wasn't just her.

What had any of these women done? What had any of them done to deserve this?

She suppressed a growl at the image of Garnier, burnt on the back of her eyelids. If she ever made it out of here alive, she'd make sure he received a good beating.

Her heart hammered at the thought, a smile spreading, then a frown as she realized how evil her thoughts were turning. It was a side of her she had never seen before, and it scared her.

Could the priest be right? Could she actually be possessed, and just not know it? She had heard him speak of being able to see the evil that was there, even when others couldn't. Could he be right?

She sighed, refusing to believe it. She was a good person, she knew it. She was certain everyone had stray thoughts that they would never act upon. And she never would beat Garnier like she had imagined, though a good slap would do him good for being so foolish.

Then a tear formed in the corner of her eye, immediately freezing, as she thought of the cost that had already been paid.

The life of her friend.

And it killed her that she didn't know which one to pray for.

Oh God, please save us!

De Rancourt Residence

Crécy-la-Chapelle, Kingdom of France

Lady Joanne stared out at the storm, the children sitting around the table with her chambermaid Beatrice, their mastiff, Tanya, whimpering at the door. Joanne patted her on the head, the poor girl staring up at her for a moment before returning her attention to what lay beyond the door.

It was unlike her to be without her master, once the late Sir Henri, and now the new arrival, Sir Marcus, but when Marcus and Simon had left for Paris, he had ordered her to stay, and in the haste of David's departure for the great city to the west, he had ordered her to stay as well.

Tanya was unhappy, to say the least.

A knock at the door brought all their activity to a halt, Beatrice breaking the silence.

"Who in their right mind would be out in this?"

Joanne shook her head. "A fool for sure." She raised her voice. "Who is it?"

"It's me, Garnier!"

"A fool it is." She opened the door and Tanya bolted. Joanne rushed out after the beast, but there would be no stopping the girl. "Get back here you stupid hound! You'll freeze to death!"

But she was ignored, as expected, the dog already at the end of the laneway that led from the farm, and in the failing light, appeared to head in the direction Jeremy and David had two nights before.

She cursed then stepped inside, hauling Garnier in by the collar. She closed the door and shook off the snow before assessing the fool. "What business do you have here after what you've done?"

Garnier's eyes were red, directed at the floor, his hands clasping and unclasping in front of him, his shoulders rounded inward. "I-I've come to apologize."

"You're lucky I don't knife you right here and feed you to the animals!" cried Beatrice, holding up the knife she was using to chop vegetables.

Garnier's eyes widened and he took a step back, probably having underestimated the level of hostility he was to expect. "I'm sorry, I know I have no right to expect you to accept my apology, but I've also come to offer my assistance in any way I can."

Joanne grunted, returning to her chair. "We have four Templars looking for her. Do you think *you* can do better?"

He shook his head, his eyes wide. "Never could I dream of being as capable as them. What I meant was, with them gone, perhaps there is some work around the farm that I could do in their absence?"

Joanne paused, exchanging a look with Beatrice who shrugged, her expression suggesting she too thought it might be a good idea. Joanne turned back to Garnier. "You're right, there is. The animals need tending to, and the stable and barn need cleaning."

Garnier's face brightened. "I'll see to it right away."

Joanne was tempted to let him do so as penance for what the jealous fool had done, but she was a good Christian. "No. Come in the morning. Your parents will be worried sick about you out in this storm."

He bowed deeply. "Thank you, m'Lady. I will be here at first light."

"You do that."

Garnier left with a spring in his step, and Joanne took one last look outside for Tanya before closing the door. She frowned at Beatrice. "Well, I think that's the last we'll see of that stupid dog."

Beatrice's eyebrows rose. "I thought calling the poor boy names was what got us all into this situation in the first place."

Joanne stared at her chambermaid for a moment, confused, then laughed. "Tanya, you smartass, Tanya!"

Durant Residence

Paris, Kingdom of France

Marcus rolled over onto his back, groaning as he tried to figure out what had woken him. Sun was pouring in through the windows and the gaps in the wood, suggesting an end to the storm that had shaken the home all night.

A knock at the door answered his question.

Simon growled, pushing to his feet as he let loose a stream of curses that would make a fishmonger blush. He opened the door and Sir Denys entered, appearing none the worse for wear.

"What, you're all still asleep?"

Marcus pushed to his feet, stretching, his crusty old sergeant delivering the reply he wanted to himself.

"We didn't have the benefit of thick walls and servants to provide us comfort."

Denys laughed. "This is true! I sometimes forget how difficult life must be for those without means. Tonight, should you still be in the city, you will stay with me."

Marcus shook his head, nodding at Thomas who entered from the back, having had the luxury of sleeping in his own bed. "Master Thomas' home is sufficient, thank you." He glanced about to be certain of what he already knew. "David didn't return last night, so we must begin a search."

Denys frowned. "That could take some time."

Marcus agreed. "I don't see that we have a choice. How does it look outside?"

"A fine winter's day. The snow has stopped, the sky is blue, the sun is warm on the skin, and the filth that is Paris has been hidden away for at least a few hours by a lovely blanket of snow."

"Someone's in a good mood," growled Simon.

"Yes, yes, I am. Thanks to you, my friends, I once again have a purpose. Last night was the first night I went to bed sober in weeks if not months, and today is the first day I haven't woken with a pounding headache. Life is good, and I intend to enjoy it to the fullest."

Another knock at the door had a smiling Denys opening with a flourish. Two women entered, confused, their faces brightening at the familiar Thomas.

"We've brought you gentlemen breakfast. I hope you don't mind."

Simon leaned toward the baskets, steam rising from beneath the cloth covering them. "I don't think there's a man alive who would mind being brought food. Especially food that smells so good."

Thomas took the baskets, bowing his head. "Thank you, it is

appreciated, but again, not necessary."

Both women bowed their way out the door, insisting it was, Denys closing the door behind them with a smile. "See, a wonderful day!"

Thomas stoked the fire, the house slowly warming as they tucked into the delicious food. Marcus would have preferred to get underway immediately, though there was no denying that a full stomach would go a long way to making their efforts a little easier in the hours ahead.

But with each passing minute, his concern for David's well-being continued to increase.

Saint-Julien Church

Outskirts of Paris, Kingdom of France

David's body ached from having been beaten repeatedly yesterday, his only reprieve the fact the monks delivering the blows decided their own sleep was of more importance than his interrogation, an interrogation that had failed. He had stuck to his story of merely seeking shelter in the storm, and despite their best efforts to get him to admit he was actually looking for them, he was convinced that at least some of them believed him.

And that these weren't the same monks he and Jeremy had encountered two days ago, but were almost definitely part of the same order.

If they were monks at all.

The fact they didn't speak like monks was the first indication, the blasphemous things spewing from their mouths as they interrogated him requiring a lengthy confession. The fact they would beat an innocent man, especially one wearing Templar markings, was another. But it was the swords that they carried, just like those monks he and Jeremy had confronted, that told him they were associated with the priest's group, and that they likely weren't monks at all.

What had the priest said?

"The kind that deal with demons, and those that would follow them."

Again with the demons. If it were for show, then why were these monks armed, and so on edge? Were these monks truly battling Satan's minions? Was Isabelle just an innocent taken by mistake? Or was something more sinister at play?

Nothing he had seen, either that night with Jeremy, or here as their captive, gave any indication these men didn't believe what the priest had said. Their intense questioning during the beating last night left little doubt they were desperate to know if they had been discovered. That level of paranoia had to mean something.

There was one way he could find out for certain if these were the monks they were searching for.

Name the priest.

It would confirm two things.

First, if they recognized the name, then he'd know that Hugo Mercier was indeed who they were seeking, and that the man who had taken Isabelle was indeed not a priest.

And second, if they recognized the name, then he had found where they were taking Isabelle, and their search was over.

Unfortunately, mentioning Mercier's name would confirm to his captors that he had indeed been looking for them, and that they had been discovered, and it would likely mean his immediate execution.

And even if they did keep him alive for some reason, he'd never escape, and there would never be any way to inform Sir Marcus of his discovery.

His only hope was rescue. From the sound of things, the storm had broken, though the cold hadn't. His hands and feet had been bound before he had been tossed in a corner as far from the fire as possible. He was nearly frozen, his entire body trembling, his only reprieve a patch of sunlight currently on his chest, shining through a hole in the roof, the warmth welcoming.

But it was hope that was providing the fire that would keep him alive. Hope brought on by the sunlight, and the knowledge that it meant his master and the others would now be searching for him. They would know something had gone wrong, and it was likely at one of the churches he was tasked to investigate. Marcus would lead them on a search, in numbers so as the same thing wouldn't happen to another that had happened to him, and they would eventually find this place and save him.

He stared at the monks, all asleep near the fire, willing them to remain that way for as long as possible. Marcus and the others, he was sure, would have been up at the crack of dawn, with the search already well underway. If his friends could find this place and surprise the monks in their sleep, then nobody on the right side of this conflict would be hurt.

One of the monks stirred, and his heart sank.

I guess it's to be a fight.

He just hoped that he was around to see it, for he feared that with no one else showing up overnight, the monks might decide he was telling the truth, that he had merely been seeking shelter, and dispatch him with haste and without a second thought.

His stomach rumbled as the first of those to wake prepared a hearty meal over the fire, the aromas reaching him in the far corner, and as his hunger pangs grew stronger, he knew none of what was being prepared would be given to him.

Why feed the condemned man?

The doors burst open and a monk he didn't recognize rushed in, followed by two who had evidently been on guard duty outside. Those not awake scrambled to their feet in short order.

"Change of plans. They'll be here later today."

A round of curses erupted before the man apparently in charge responded. "Why? What's happened?"

"There may be trouble on the route. We were forced to kill some nosy Templar, so Father Mercier thought it best to return early and perform the exorcisms before the guy's partner found us."

"You killed a Templar?"

"Yeah, just a squire. Not a knight."

The leader jabbed a thumb over his shoulder at David. "A Templar squire like this one?"

The new arrival's eyes bulged and he strode quickly over to David, kicking him onto his back with his boot. "I recognize you!" He cursed, turning to the others. "Where did you find him?"

"Snooping around outside. You mean this is the other's partner?"

"Yes. This one and his friend confronted us a couple of nights ago and tried to get back one of the girls. They retreated as soon as we presented our swords, the cowards."

David bit his tongue as his chest ached with the news that Jeremy was dead. He wanted to lash out at these vile murderers, but he was bound, hand and feet, and useless.

The man kicked him in the side then headed for the front of the church, their conversation resuming, though this time in hushed tones. The new arrival soon left, the sound of his horse galloping off convincing David that if he managed to survive the next few minutes, it would only be a short reprieve until the man returned with instructions to kill him as well.

I'll be with you soon, my friend.

Outside Coulommiers, Kingdom of France

Jeremy wasn't sure if he was alive. He couldn't open his eyes or even move a muscle in his frozen body, though he could feel something on his face, and hear something in the distance.

A dog barking.

It was getting closer, the incessant bark almost annoying now.

And familiar.

Tanya!

He willed himself to open his eyes, yet failed, then he felt something running over his face, over his eyelids, something warm and wet, then another bark, this time right in front of him.

It *was* Tanya.

She was here, with him, wherever here was. It couldn't be Hell, for it was too cold, and it couldn't be Heaven for the same reason—he

164

imagined a balmier climate than this in paradise.

He was alive.

He had to be.

But how was Tanya here? The dog licked his eyes again, and he struggled to open them once more, this time succeeding, if only slightly. He coughed suddenly, taking a deep breath, an icy chill filling his body as reality rushed back to crush any fantasies he might have had of being home where Tanya should be.

He was in the abandoned barn he had found in the storm. His fire was long out, his horse was standing in the far corner, looking none the worse for wear, and Tanya was in front of him, panting with as happy an expression on her face as he had yet to see.

"Y-you found me, girl."

She shoved her snout under his chin and he chuckled, though still found himself frozen in place.

But she felt warm.

Very warm.

He forced his arm up, raising his blanket. "Get in here, girl."

Tanya complied, and Jeremy's arm dropped over the massive dog as she pushed back into him, her body heat soon having an effect on him. As he lay there, taking slow, steady breaths, and moving his fingers and toes as best he could, the warmth from the large mastiff flowed through him, and in what felt like perhaps an hour, though was hopefully far less, he was able to move most of his body.

And that meant a fire was in order.

He lifted the blanket and Tanya jumped up, rushing around the barn excitedly as if she knew she had done a good thing. With some effort, his numb trembling hands anything but cooperative, he started a fire, and using scrap boards from the collapsing barn, he had a good-sized one going within minutes, its warmth enough to finish the job Tanya had started of warming his bones, as well as those of his companions, his horse drawing near immediately, Tanya sitting by Jeremy's side, leaning against him.

His hands were feeling near normal now, though his fingertips were still stinging as if hundreds of needles were being jabbed into them. His toes were still numb, and he thanked God he had apparently had the presence of mind in the middle of the night to take some rocks from the fire and put them under his blanket to keep his feet warm.

It had probably saved them.

He touched the tip of his nose and winced. He pulled his knife and used the blade to examine his reflection. His nose was white when he touched it, but it slowly would turn pink again if left alone. It would appear that whatever had happened to his extremities had also happened to his nose.

He stood, stomping his feet for a few moments, then began walking around in the barn, loosening himself up. He stretched then gasped in pain as his ribs, numbed from the frigid temperature, reminded him that they were broken.

He collapsed to one knee, Tanya instantly at his side. He took several slow, tentative breaths, then nodded at the girl. "I'm okay. I'll just have to remember I'm injured." He pushed to his feet and packed his horse, though not before feeding her with supplies he had brought from the commandry.

They were soon underway, though he had lost at least a couple of hours of daylight. With the weather now good, he should make Paris by nightfall then find Sir Marcus. He would know what to do about

166

Isabelle.

A jolt of pain rocked him, as if his ribs were punishing him for his failure. He pressed a hand against them and urged his horse on quicker.

Then cursed at the sight of a town not two hundred paces ahead. A town he hadn't seen in the storm. He cursed again, thinking of how much better his circumstances might have been if he had only made it a little farther last night.

He made for a livery stable, quickly arranging for his horse to be properly tended to, then surveyed the town. "You wouldn't have noticed a group come through here perhaps late yesterday, maybe this morning, led by a priest?"

The man's eyes widened. "A priest? Can't say that I did, though I've been busy in the back most of the morning." He pointed across the street. "Check with Mrs. Desprez at the inn. She seems to notice everything that happens in this town, even the things she has no business noticing."

Jeremy smiled slightly. "Does she serve good food?"

The man shrugged. "It'll be hot, which from the looks of you is all I think you need." He pointed at Jeremy's nose. "You best be wearing something to cover your face a little better, or you're going to get frostbite."

Jeremy's eyes narrowed. "Frostbite? What's that?"

The man slapped Jeremy's Templar surcoat. "They don't make you Templars very smart, do they?"

Jeremy chuckled. "I'm afraid I've been in the Holy Land most of my life. This is my first winter."

The man laughed. "I suppose it's been quite the shock to you, hey?"

Jeremy grunted. "You have no idea." He touched his nose. "So, tell me of this frostbite. What can it do?"

"If you let your fingers or toes, or your nose or ears, get too cold for too long, they'll turn black and pretty much drop off."

"My Lord!" Jeremy made the sign of the cross, silently apologizing for his blasphemous outburst. "How do you protect against it?"

The man shrugged as if it were obvious. "Keep dry, dress in layers, and keep the extremities warm. Have your feet as close to the fire as you safely can, sleep with your face and ears covered, and tuck your hands under your armpits or between your legs where your little man resides. Don't worry, you'll get used to it eventually."

Jeremy frowned. "I hope so." He shook the man's hand. "Thanks for the advice." He pointed at Tanya. "Can I leave her here? I'm not sure if she'll be welcome at the inn."

"She won't, and you can. I'll feed her for you."

Jeremy smiled. "Thanks." He turned to Tanya then pointed at the forge nearby, kicking out heat. "Stay. I'll be back soon."

She whimpered, clearly not pleased, but headed for the warmth of the fire, curling up beside it. Jeremy headed across the road and entered the inn, finding only one other customer there, most of the travelers probably already long gone.

"What do you want?" asked a cranky looking woman behind a large cauldron in the far corner.

Jeremy smiled. "A warm meal and some conversation?"

She filled a bowl with a thick, hearty helping of porridge then a cup with a pale wine. He sat at the long table and took a tentative taste of the food. It wasn't what he had come to expect at the farm, but it was edible, more so in his current state. He attacked it with gusto, and was almost finished when he noticed her staring at him, a grin on her face.

"You forgot about the conversation."

He laughed. "I guess I didn't realize how hungry I was."

She held up another heavy spoonful. "More?"

"Please." He slid his bowl toward her and it was quickly refilled. He continued to eat, slower this time, then leaned closer to the woman. "Did you happen to see a group go through here this morning, perhaps late yesterday, led by a priest?"

The woman's eyes narrowed. "An odd question, that. Why, did he do something to upset the Templars?"

Jeremy forced a laugh, not wanting her to think anything untoward had happened. "Nothing of the sort. I have a message for the Father, and I'm afraid I got a little lost in the storm. I just want to know if I'm on the right track."

She regarded him for a moment then finally nodded. "He and a bunch of monks ate here this morning. I guess they camped outside of town. They left a couple of hours ago."

"Did they say where they were going?"

"Paris, I believe."

Jeremy's heart pounded. "Any idea where? I mean, it's a big city to try and find him in."

She shook her head. "No idea." She paused. "Wait, I heard him say something about getting back to the church." She eyed him. "Surely you know what church he preaches at?"

Jeremy lied with a nod. "Of course. If I don't catch up to him on the road, then I'll find him there." He finished his meal then reached into his pocket to retrieve a coin for payment.

The woman shook her head. "No man who serves God pays for his meal here."

He smiled gratefully at her. "You're a good woman, madam. I'll pray for you tonight."

A cackle erupted from her. "I'm beyond saving, Templar, but you go ahead and try!"

En route to Paris, Kingdom of France

Father Mercier sighed as he stared up at the bright blue sky. "It's a beautiful day, a beautiful day to do God's work, isn't it?"

"It is indeed."

"When we get to the church, I think I'll do the Lost Cause first. She's usually good for a day or two, and since she's been through this so often, she's good with the others after they've been saved."

"She'll be able to keep them calm until you get them back home."

Mercier sighed. "I pray that one day we can save her poor wretched soul too, but for some reason, Satan has sunk his claws deeply in her. I wonder why that is."

"Perhaps she has done something so evil in her past, perhaps before she was possessed, that God had forsaken her."

Mercier nodded. "That's possible, I suppose, though Jesus forgave us for all our sins. Does she not deserve the same? Does she not deserve a chance at redemption, to save her soul from eternal damnation?"

"I would think so, but who am I to doubt the Lord?"

Mercier chuckled. "Who indeed? And here I sit, doing the very same thing." He sighed. "I believe she is my cross to bear, yet another burden placed upon my shoulders by the Holy Spirit himself. The day I finally save her soul, is the day I can finally rest. But until that day, *she* is His message to me that my work is not yet done."

One of his men pointed ahead. "Father, we're almost there!"

He stood from his seat, the reins still in his hands, and smiled as the city he called home appeared on the horizon, a den of depravity if there ever was one, but still his home. He glanced over his shoulder at those about to be saved, snarling and growling behind him, and smiled.

"Don't worry, you sweet things. You will soon be saved then returned to your loved ones, I promise."

The Lost Cause barked at him, and he smiled.

"Even you, some day."

A horse approached, the rider hailing him by name, and he frowned as he recognized the man.

"What is it, brother?"

"We might have a problem."

Saint-Julien Church

Outskirts of Paris, Kingdom of France

David sat in the corner, ignored, freezing, his stomach still rumbling, none of the food, as expected, shared with him. The messenger had left several hours ago, and depending upon where this Father Mercier was, could be back at any moment with orders to kill him. All he could hope was that the delay meant his friends might find him before those orders arrived.

He took little comfort in finally confirming that these monks were indeed connected to those who had kidnapped Isabelle. There couldn't possibly be two Father Mercier's traveling with armed monks. It was a vital piece of information Sir Marcus needed to know, yet barring a miracle, he could see no way in which to inform his master.

So, he waited. And while he waited, he hated to admit that what he was witnessing was fascinating. The monks were clearly preparing for a ritual, suggesting there would be no delay for rest after Mercier arrived.

A table had been set up, restraints at either end suggesting it was meant to be some sort of altar atop which people would be held. A deep purple cloth covered it, and dozens of crosses were placed on the floor, surrounding the table, as if they were guardians, the base of each pointing away from the center. If an exorcism was indeed to be performed here, then he had a feeling these crosses were meant to keep any additional evil spirits out of whomever they were trying to save. Torches were lit all around the area, casting a gentle yellow and orange glow to the entire interior, revealing just how horrid a state this church was in.

There's no way a real priest would preach out of here.

From what he had been told, Mercier was not an ordained priest, had been kicked out of the University of Paris several years ago, and never heard from since. This church was on the list of abandoned ones, so clearly nothing had changed in the man's status.

He was still insane.

At least that was David's opinion of him. He had to be. Right? He thought all beautiful women were possessed by demons in service to Satan himself, and traveled around kidnaping them, and exorcising those demons.

And though David had failed, and so too Jeremy, he did hold out some small hope that in the end, Isabelle might be okay. Mercier had said she would be returned once cleansed, and these monks were definitely preparing for a ritual the likes of which he had never seen.

It was disturbing.

The men were all moving with purpose, everything done with precision, as if they took their duties seriously. And if this were a farce, would they be so diligent? Isabelle wasn't possessed, yet these men acted as if what they were doing truly was the work of the Lord.

It had him wondering what was actually going on here. If these monks, these monks like no other he had encountered outside of the Order, did indeed believe in what they were doing, as Father Mercier certainly seemed to, could Isabelle merely be a mistake?

His heart raced with the prospect. If this had all simply been a mistake, a misunderstanding, and Mercier and these monks were indeed good men doing the work of the Lord, then perhaps Isabelle had been safe all along, and once the error was discovered, she would be handed over to him, safe and sound.

The front doors burst open once again, the messenger, gasping for breath, having returned.

"I have new instructions."

Approaching Saint-Julien Church
Outskirts of Paris, Kingdom of France

Marcus eyed the church ahead, Saint-Julien another on David's list. It had been hours, and though they hadn't found him yet, they were at least eliminating possibilities—though that assumed his squire was in one of the churches, and the more he thought about it, the more he thought that was unlikely. Surely, he would have sought refuge in one of the many houses or businesses that dotted the outskirts of the great city.

Inquiries at these places had so far proven fruitless and time-consuming, though they were necessary. A note had been left for David with strict instructions to remain at Thomas' should he return, or head for the Fortress if he were in danger.

He had a suspicion this search would prove a waste of time, and that they'd find David eating another pie from a grateful neighbor when they returned. He smiled at the thought.

Simon grunted. "What could you possibly be smiling about? Aren't you as miserable as the rest of us?"

Marcus chuckled. "I was just thinking how David is probably sitting by the fire back at Thomas' house, while we freeze out here looking for him."

Simon growled. "If that proves to be true, I'm going to kill him myself."

Marcus laughed, then after a moment, frowned. "You do realize that David *is* probably safe somewhere, and that we have made no progress on finding Isabelle? None of these churches we have examined so far have shown any evidence of organized activity."

Denys gestured at the church ahead. "How many of these are left from David's map?"

"Just another handful."

Simon pointed. "Is that smoke?"

Marcus peered into the bright landscape then nodded as he spotted a wisp of smoke rising lazily into the sky above the church, the wind almost still. He urged his horse forward. "Let's hope it's David."

Simon agreed. "Yes, let's. Then we throw him on the fire so we can warm ourselves."

Marcus smiled at his friend, whose determined expression suggested he might not be entirely joking.

Saint-Chapelle Church

Outskirts of Paris, Kingdom of France

Isabelle watched in horror as the woman she had heard referred to as the Lost Cause writhed and hissed on the altar. A fire roared to their left as dozens of torches lit the entire proceedings. Crosses were set about the altar, and the monks all stood around it, chanting something in Latin repeatedly, their fervor growing with each recitation.

The priest, Father Mercier, circled the woman, waving a thurible over her body, the wisps of incense filling the air as he read from the Bible, his words lost on her as well.

And the woman.

The woman was terrifying.

As she struggled against the bonds holding her, her back would arch, and she appeared at times to lift from the table, the four monks

178

at each corner struggling to hold her down. Her growls and barks were chilling, though it was the guttural words she continually spat while glaring at poor Father Mercier, that had Isabelle nearly sick with fear for not only herself, but him as well.

For this *was* evil.

There was no doubt of that. She was now convinced that Father Mercier was doing the Lord's work, and these monks were as well. And though she wasn't possessed, this woman clearly was. Her soul needed saving, though if they were calling her the Lost Cause, then she must have been through this before.

Isabelle shuddered. What would happen when they dragged her onto the altar and began their ritual? What would happen when she didn't respond like this one? Would they keep trying? Would they think she was a lost cause as well? Would they keep her locked up forever, like they had this one, because they could never save her?

She nearly fainted at the thought.

Maybe I should fake it.

It was a terrifying idea, though if she acted like this one, then abruptly stopped, perhaps Mercier would believe she had been saved, and would let her go.

She sobbed along with the others, none of whom to her seemed at all anything but normal. None of these women were possessed. None of them. Could the priest have made a mistake with all of them? And why were they all so beautiful? She knew she was pretty, though these women were far more beautiful than she was, or at least felt she was.

Yet this was why they were here, wasn't it? That their beauty was a sign of the Devil's hand at play?

She returned to her earlier troubled thoughts. Could she be

possessed and just not know it? Her stomach flipped and bile filled her mouth at the prospect.

It can't be! It can't be possible!

Her entire body shook with fear. Not with fear of what was about to happen, but fear of what she might be.

Suddenly Father Mercier held his wooden cross high over his head, the monks yelling their incantations now, the priest red and covered in sweat, before he dropped it hard on the woman's chest. She screamed in agony, arching her back, writhing in pain before collapsing. He repeated his prayer, then dropped it once more, eliciting another scream and frenzied resistance before collapse. And then a third time, the woman's rage guttural, agonized, and finally understood.

"I will be back!"

She collapsed, her chest heaving from exhaustion, then she looked about, finally staring up at Father Mercier. And the sweetest voice gasped out a question.

"Oh no, Father, did it happen again?"

Mercier patted her cheek. "I'm afraid so, my child." He signaled to the monks, and they quickly undid her bonds then helped her to a seated position. "How do you feel?"

She smiled. "Good." Her smiled broadened. "Myself." She shuddered. "And I remember everything that it made me do." Tears rolled down her cheeks. "I'm so sorry, Father."

He put an arm over her shoulders. "It's not your fault, my child." He helped her to her feet and handed her off to two monks who had been standing to the side of the ritual. "Take her. Give her food and water, and fresh clothes. Is the bath ready?"

"Almost. The move delayed us, unfortunately."

Mercier waved a hand at their surroundings. "Nothing to worry about. I've always liked Saint-Chapelle, and it won't delay God's work." He pointed at Isabelle and her bladder released, a warm stream of shame rushing down her legs.

"Bring her."

Saint-Julien Church

Outskirts of Paris, Kingdom of France

Marcus crept closer to the church, listening for any sign that whoever had set the dying fire was still there, but hearing nothing beyond the footsteps of his companions, crunching on the snow. How anyone could sneak up on another during winter was beyond him, the desert sand he was accustomed to always quiet.

He reached a window and peered through the gaps in the shutters, seeing nothing but the glow of the embers that remained. Simon, at the window on the opposite side of the doors, shook his head, indicating he too saw nothing. Marcus glanced over his shoulder to make sure Thomas was safely out of the way, and he smiled awkwardly back at him as he held the reins of the horses, no doubt feeling ashamed he was not taking part in the altercation that might be about to happen.

Marcus hauled open the door and Simon charged inside. Marcus followed along with Sir Denys, and they spread out, finding the church empty as Marcus had suspected and feared.

"David!"

Simon rushed to the rear of the church, and Marcus followed as soon as he spotted a tied up bundle in the corner, recognizing his squire at once. Simon pulled his dagger, slicing the ropes binding their friend.

Marcus knelt, examining his loyal squire, the man clearly having been beaten badly, his face swollen and bloodied. "What did they do to you, my friend?"

David leaned against the wall. "You should see how they look."

Marcus smiled, wit a good sign one didn't fear death. He turned back toward the door. "Thomas, food and water!"

"Okay!"

The young man rushed in moments later with the requested items, and David gratefully drank the water, ravenously devouring the provisions.

Simon grunted. "I'd suspect they didn't feed you, but I've seen you eat on a normal day, and it doesn't look much different."

David grunted then offered Simon some of the food. "Is that your way of saying you're hungry too?"

Simon roared with laughter, smacking David on the shoulder. "You'll live." He hauled David to his feet, their squire still shoveling food into his mouth with one hand, and drink with the other, as they led him toward the still warm hearth.

"Tell us, what happened here?"

David dropped to the floor, exhausted, and they joined him, Thomas tossing onto the fire some more wood that sat nearby, poking it for several minutes, his efforts quickly rewarded, brightening David's mood considerably. "That feels so good. The bastards kept me as far from the fire as was possible, and didn't feed me or let me drink." He frowned. "And they wouldn't let me go to the bathroom."

Simon leaned in, sniffing. "You still smell like the little shit you've always been."

David reached to hit Simon then glanced at both hands, still occupied. "You're lucky I'm busy." He turned back to Marcus. "It was definitely the same group that took Isabelle, just different monks, if you know what I mean."

Marcus did. "How can you be certain?"

"Well, beyond the fact they were armed monks, a messenger arrived at first light, and he recognized me from two nights ago. Before he knew I was here, he said something about a Father Mercier."

Denys clapped. "There you go, there can't be two of them now, can there?"

David nodded. "That's what I was thinking." His face clouded. "But there's more. He said they had killed a Templar squire." His voice cracked. "It has to be Jeremy."

Marcus' chest tightened with sorrow at the news, Simon turning away to hide his own pain. Jeremy had been with Marcus for so long, he couldn't imagine that the man he had known since he was a boy, was gone, torn from their lives by these blasphemous imposters. A fire raged in his stomach, and his jaw squared. "He will be avenged."

Simon turned back to face the group. "Damned right he will be. I want them dead. All of them. Dead!"

Marcus reached out and grabbed his friend by the arm, squeezing it. "Agreed, but first we must save Isabelle and the others." He looked at David, the closest to Jeremy, and his heart ached once again at the tears that streaked their friend's cheeks. "Continue. What happened next?"

David wiped his eyes dry with the back of his hand then drew a deep, steadying breath. "The, umm, messenger, returned about an hour or two ago, I'm sorry, I've sort of lost track of time, and then they all packed up and left."

"Why didn't they kill you?"

He shrugged. "I think I heard the messenger say that Father Mercier felt it wasn't necessary, since I wouldn't know where they were going."

Marcus grunted. "What a generous man, leaving you tied up in the cold."

David swallowed. "Agreed, though I'm not sure if that was their idea or not. They didn't seem pleased to be leaving me alive."

Simon grunted. "Dissent in the ranks?"

Marcus frowned. "So, you don't know where they went."

David shook his head before motioning to the left of the door. "They went south, I think."

"We might still be able to track them, as there's been no new snow today." Marcus turned to Thomas. "I want you to take him to your home so he can recover."

Thomas flushed. "But, well, I, umm, want to be there for Isabelle."

Marcus understood the young man's desires, but he had to think what was best for the mission at hand. "Sir Denys is experienced in battle, and you are not. Having three experienced swords will improve the odds of us saving Isabelle."

Thomas' shoulders slumped. "You're right, of course."

But it was David's turn to protest. "I can still fight. An experienced archer and Thomas' eye are better than just three swords. And besides, I want to be there when you send them to Hell."

Marcus shook his head. "You're in no condition."

Simon put a hand on David's shoulder. "He's right, you'll just slow us down. Even more so than usual."

David didn't bother with a retort, realizing they were right. He sighed. "The fact I can't think of anything to say I fear proves your point." He held up his arms and Marcus and Simon hauled him to his feet. David put an arm over Thomas' shoulders. "Take me home, young one, so they can get on with the hunt and send these heathens to their eternal damnation."

Saint-Chapelle Church

Outskirts of Paris, Kingdom of France

Isabelle retreated as two monks approached her, but found her way blocked by the icy chill of the stone wall behind her. They grabbed her, each by an arm, and hauled her toward the altar slowly, deliberately, as if her own approach was part of the ritual the monks had already begun with their chanting.

The one on her left bent over and pressed his lips against her ears, and what he said stunned her. "You saw what to do. Mimic her as best you can, then I will squeeze your hand three times. He will press the cross against your chest three times. Scream on the first and second, like the other one did, then act normal on the third. It will all be over soon."

Her heart slammed against her ribcage as she struggled to not pass out, her mind a confused mess as she processed what had been said to her. The monk knew she wasn't possessed, otherwise he would never have said such things, but if he knew, then why wasn't anyone telling Father Mercier? Why were they letting this horror continue?

She was lifted and laid down on the altar, her hands and feet quickly bound, each of her wrists and ankles gripped by one of the monks who stood at the four corners of the purple covered table. She trembled with fright as she continued to struggle with what had been said.

It was fake.

But why?

Mercier obviously believed in what he was doing, and the first woman had clearly been possessed. Isabelle couldn't believe the woman had faked what she had just seen. She had elevated off the altar, she had spoken some unknown language, and the entire time she had seen her in the wagon, she had been inhuman.

How could anyone walk as she had walked, her body so contorted? It had been terrifying not only to her, but to everyone who had seen her.

No, the Lost Cause had to have been possessed.

Yet Isabelle knew she herself wasn't, and apparently so did this monk. Did the others realize the mistake made as well? Was this to save face? Was this to make Father Mercier think he hadn't made a mistake? But why? Why not just admit it?

And how could the monk know? Shouldn't the priest be the expert? And what of the others? They all seemed normal. Would they too be given the same instructions? And if so, then that would mean Mercier had made a mistake with all of them. Was this entire thing simply to humor him?

It made no sense.

The grip tightened on her arm, to the point of being painful, and she turned her head to look at the monk who had whispered her the instructions. He glared at her, and she knew what he meant. She closed her eyes, trying to picture everything that had happened only minutes ago.

And she roared.

And it even frightened her.

She roared again, twisting and turning, struggling against her bonds, then arched her back, shoving her hips off the altar and into the air. The grips on her extremities tightened, and at first, she thought it was to hold her in place, then she nearly gasped as the monks lifted her into the air, and she almost smiled as she realized what was happening.

The screams from the other girls confirmed it.

The monks were causing her to levitate off the altar, and if they were doing that, it had her wondering if they had done the same for the Lost Cause, or was this only for those mistakenly condemned by their priest. Mercier continued to encircle her, and she writhed against the monks, grunting and screaming, playing her part though saying nothing, as the only words she could think of were French or Latin, neither of which the Lost Cause had uttered.

The ritual seemed to go on forever, but it was only minutes, the entire experience, though fake, still terrifying. She had to keep up the performance, for if she didn't, she feared that the priest might think he failed.

The monk squeezed her wrist three times, her heart leaping as she realized it was almost over, and the most important part was about to begin. She glared at Mercier as the cross slapped down on her chest.

She screamed as she never had before, arching her back as she once again felt herself lifted from the table.

The cross was removed and she collapsed, continuing to writhe against those holding her, then he hit her chest once again and she howled, arching her back even harder, though this time the monks held her in place, and she readied herself for the most critical part of her act.

The cross lifted and she collapsed before it was pressed against her chest one final time. She stayed still but screamed, remembering the words that had erupted from the Lost Cause, though deciding it was best not to suggest the exorcism hadn't been a complete and total success.

"No!" was all she could think of to yell, then she collapsed, genuinely exhausted. She forced a smile as Mercier brushed the hair from her face.

"How do you feel, my child?"

She sighed. "Good. The best I think I've ever felt. What happened?"

"You were possessed by a demon in the service of the Devil." He flicked his wrist and the monks untied her. Father Mercier helped her up then pointed to where the Lost Cause had been taken earlier. "Go. There is food and drink for you, fresh clothes, and a bath."

She smiled. "Thank you." She stayed in character as best she could, and once through the door, the monks remaining on the other side, she shook, tears erupting as her ordeal might finally be over.

"Why the tears?"

She nearly jumped out of her skin at the voice, finally noticing the Lost Cause bathing herself in the far corner.

"From what I could hear, you put on a good show."

Isabelle approached her. "I don't understand. You knew?"

The woman laughed. "Of course. The man is quite mad." She pointed at a table in the corner. "Eat something, quickly, then clean yourself up. We'll be leaving shortly."

Isabelle trembled. "Wh-where are we going?"

The girl smiled at her, but there was something behind it that reminded her of their encounters in the prison wagon. "Why home, of course."

Outskirts of Paris, Kingdom of France

Sir Denys cursed. "What now?"

Marcus stared at the mess that lay in front of them. They had followed the trail left in the snow easily at first, a cart and half a dozen horses not much of a challenge in fresh snow. But soon they had intersected a road much more traveled, and the trail was quickly lost.

Yet there was still hope.

"Well, we know they were definitely heading in this direction, to the south. David said they had been preparing for a ritual, and that they left in a hurry. That can only mean they thought they were going to be discovered."

Simon grunted. "Right, by us."

"Right, because David was recognized. But they left him alive, which means they were confident we would have no idea where they were going next."

"Or they thought he would die before we found him."

Marcus shook his head. "No, I don't think they'd chance that. I think they believe they have escaped cleanly. That means they'll set up wherever they are now, probably quite secure in the false knowledge that they are safe."

Simon pursed his lips, surveying the road. "As far as our current situation is concerned, they *are* safe. We have no way of knowing where they went."

Marcus stared at the road, at least a dozen carriages heading in either direction. "You're forgetting one thing."

"What's that?"

Marcus tapped his head. "This memory of mine. You're aware we are at the southernmost section of the map that was provided us, and that there are only three more churches that they could be at."

Denys shook his head. "That assumes they've set up at a church. This could all be some clever scheme to kidnap beautiful women."

Marcus nodded. "True, but you're forgetting one thing."

Denys' eyes narrowed. "What's that?"

"David said the monks were preparing for a ritual. You don't do that if this is all just a ruse. Clearly, Father Mercier is going to perform an exorcism, and if he is, he'll want to do it in a church."

Simon frowned. "I'm afraid I'm not as confident as you."

Marcus smiled. "That's because you are far stupider than I am."

Simon chuckled. "It is a constant state of awe that I find myself in when I bear witness to your greatness."

"I'm glad you recognize my superior intellect. If you didn't, I'd fear you were too stupid to remain in my company."

Denys grinned at Simon.

Simon eyed him. "What are you smiling at?"

"Apparently, an idiot."

Simon raised a finger. "That may be, but clearly not a *complete* idiot!"

Saint-Chapelle Church

Outskirts of Paris, Kingdom of France

Isabelle shivered as she slipped her feet back into her shoes, still damp after her attempts to brush them clean. She sighed and smiled, leaning her head back and closing her eyes as she felt human for the first time in days.

The sound of the door opening had her flinching, her new state of calm precarious at best. It was Annette, her eyes wide, her expression confused, her ritual apparently much like Isabelle's. She stared at Isabelle who leaped to her feet and rushed forward. She gave Annette a hug, then whispered in her ear.

"Pretend it was real."

She still didn't trust the Lost Cause. Something was going on here, something that didn't make sense, and until she was safely at her parents' house, she wouldn't believe her ordeal was over. She pointed at the table.

"Eat something quickly, then wash yourself. There are clothes over there. The next girl will probably be here in ten minutes, so you'll want to be sure you're done."

Annette nodded, her eyes still wide with confusion, then even wider at the sight of food. She attacked the offerings as the Lost Cause sat in the corner on a bench, a leg up in an unladylike fashion, watching Annette with a smile.

What was her story? Why was she different? Why was her exorcism real?

Isabelle's heart hammered with the questions, and she turned toward the door, her back to the Lost Cause, as a thought occurred to her. What made her think the exorcism was real? The fact she levitated? That had been faked during her own exorcism, the monks merely gripping her arms and legs and lifting her into the air when she arched her back and shoved her hips upward. Could they have done the same with the wretched creature they called the Lost Cause?

She pursed her lips then shook her head. The conditions had been torturous on the road, and the Lost Cause had been there apparently from the beginning, repeatedly, as her exorcism failed each time. There was no way anyone would voluntarily do that. She had to be afflicted as Father Mercier thought she was.

And there had been caring there. Compassion. The man had truly been gentle and attentive to her after the ritual had been completed, and she was a changed woman. Could the distrust Isabelle now felt be a sign that the exorcism was already failing? That the demon was reasserting control?

She turned when she heard Annette head for the water, now tepid, the room they were in cold with no fire beyond some torches. At least there was no wind, and the door to the outside seemed solid enough. She turned away, giving the poor woman her privacy, though the Lost Cause continued to ogle her. She wanted to lash out at the woman, but resisted for some reason. If she couldn't be trusted, then she was part of whatever this was, or she truly was possessed, and once the demon reasserted itself, they'd be locked in a room alone with her.

She trembled.

Or shivered.

Which, she wasn't sure. A shout from the other side of the door had her heart leaping.

Did they say someone was coming?

Outside Saint-Chapelle Church
Outskirts of Paris, Kingdom of France

These weren't the wisps of an abandoned, dying fire Marcus was looking at, but the indicators of a strong, stoked blaze within the walls of the abandoned church they now found themselves approaching. Clearly there was activity inside, though they didn't need the fire to tell them that—loud chanting echoed from inside, the eerie sound of a chorus of voices rolling across the snow-covered land chilling.

"Behind the trees, on the left," whispered Simon.

Marcus shifted his focus without moving his head, spotting the movement that Simon was referring to. He frowned. This was where a skilled archer like David or Jeremy would come in handy, though they didn't have that luxury today. Today, they would have to storm the position. They would be victorious, he had little doubt, but any hope of surprising those inside would be lost.

"Keep going," he muttered, his lips barely moving. The three of them continued past the church, a church in much better condition than where they had found David, but closer to the city, therefore perhaps not the location men performing rituals without the blessing of the Church would find ideal.

As they put the church behind them, continuing along what appeared to be a rarely traveled path, Marcus' mind raced as to what to do. The three of them, storming the church, with possibly a dozen or more armed men inside was foolish, and he wasn't prepared to lose any more of his men today.

He sighed. "We need more men."

Simon grunted. "By the time we get them, they'll be gone. It would be almost two hours before we could get a contingent from the Fortress."

Marcus frowned. "You're right, of course."

Simon smiled. "Not such an idiot after all, huh?"

Marcus laughed. "Yet still…"

Denys, silent most of the way, the cold not agreeing with him, and no stake in the events so far, finally spoke. "The palace guard."

Marcus turned to him. "What?"

"The King's Personal Guard at the palace." He pointed to the walls of the palace not fifteen minutes' ride from where they stood. "Surely, we could get a contingent to help us, considering we believe Lord Allard's daughter might be inside."

Marcus cursed himself. "I was so consumed with the thought of Isabelle, I had forgotten about her."

Simon eyed him. "So that memory isn't infallible."

Marcus shot him a look then returned his attention to Denys. "You should go alone. And make no mention of us. If they think Templars are involved at all, they might just sacrifice Lord Allard's daughter to make us look bad."

Denys nodded. "Good thinking." He urged his steed forward, and was soon galloping toward the castle walls. Simon turned to Marcus.

"What now? Memory games?"

Marcus chuckled. "You'd lose." He sighed, surveying the area. "For now, let's just keep an eye on that church and make sure they don't go anywhere."

Outskirts of Paris, Kingdom of France

They had ridden mostly in silence, David racked with guilt at having left his best friend behind to die. It was his orders that had left Jeremy trailing a dozen armed men, alone. It was idiocy. They both should have left and sought out Sir Marcus. He would have likely been able to use the Templar messenger network to find the priest and his minions, then sent cavalry to free Isabelle and the others.

Instead, he had made the foolish decision to leave his friend behind, and he had been discovered and killed.

A tear rolled down his cheek.

"Are you okay?"

He quickly wiped it away, ashamed Thomas had seen him at his weakest. "I will be, in time."

"I never thought I'd stop crying when I lost my father, but time does heal even the deepest of wounds."

David drew a deep breath, steadying himself. "Do you still mourn him?"

Thomas nodded. "Every day, though with less intensity on some days, and those days are growing in number. I'll always miss him, as I still do my mother, but I'm starting to dwell on the better times more often than the bad."

David imagined Jeremy, laughing at some foolishness, and smiled. "We did have a lot of good times. Too many to count."

"In time you'll think of those, and hopefully a smile will replace the tears."

David sighed. "In time, I suppose." He spotted a tavern ahead for weary travelers, and made a decision. He couldn't leave Marcus and Simon alone out there, he couldn't risk losing another friend. He simply needed to fortify himself against the cold, enough that he could be the archer he feared they so desperately needed. He pointed. "Let's go inside."

Thomas' eyes widened. "But Sir Marcus said to go back to my home."

"He did, and we will. But I feel weak and need sustenance and a fire now, not in half an hour."

Thomas frowned then reluctantly agreed. "Fine."

They tied up their horses then went inside, a good crowd warming up before entering the city to conduct their business. They sat as close to the fire as they could after those inside got over the surprise at his Templar surcoat and swollen face, and David soon found himself warming up. They were quickly served, and he shoved spoonful after spoonful of the stew in his mouth, drinking as much as he could hold before eying Thomas' untouched meal.

"Not hungry?"

Thomas shook his head. "I had a good breakfast."

"Lucky." David motioned toward the bowl. "May I?"

Thomas pushed the bowl toward him and it was finished off in silence. David leaned back, belched, eliciting a roar of approval from the men around them, then patted his stomach.

"I feel like a new man."

Thomas smiled slightly. "That's good. If we leave now, we can get home before the warmth from this fire wears off completely."

David shook his head. "No, we're going back to find Sir Marcus."

"But he said—"

David cut him off. "I know what he said, but if he knew how good I now feel, he never would have issued those orders. I'm feeling fine now, and I can't let them fight those people alone. There's simply too many. I'm fit enough. I just need a bow and some arrows." He surveyed the crowd and smiled. "Do you have money?"

Thomas nodded. "I do."

David pointed at a man sitting nearby with the required equipment. "Make him an offer he can't refuse."

Approaching Paris, Kingdom of France

Jeremy gripped his side, the agony unbearable despite the cold taking some of the edge off his pain. The constant motion of the horse as he urged her toward Paris was simply too much to bear anymore, and he slowed her down. Tanya, ahead, stopped as well then barked, pointing her snout forward, then turning back toward Jeremy, as if urging him onward.

"Just give me a few minutes, girl."

But the dog was insistent, continuing to bark. Jeremy growled, the barking getting on his nerves, and signaled his horse forward once more. They were soon beside the insistent mastiff, and Jeremy was about to scold her when he smiled at the sight ahead.

Paris.

He sighed, his shoulders slumping, his ribs once again protesting.

"We're almost there." He patted his horse. "Let's just push through, and we'll be at the Fortress in an hour."

They continued forward, though at a slower gait, the pain simply too much. He feared it might overwhelm him at any moment if he weren't careful.

And then he'd be of no help, though of what help he could be in his current state, he did not know. He just knew he had to reach his master and friends, before he finally succumbed.

Palais de la Cité
Paris, Kingdom of France

Sir Denys galloped through the main gates of the palace, the guards manning the entrance recognizing his family crest. He spotted the most senior guard on duty and rode over to him.

"I need two dozen men assembled immediately."

The man's eyes bulged momentarily before he recovered his composure. "Under whose authority?"

"Mine."

The man stared at him. "But you have no authority in this matter. Only the King's—"

"This is a matter of life or death. The life of Lord Allard's missing daughter is at stake." He jabbed the man's chest. "You *will* assemble the men as I have ordered, while I go inside and have your orders confirmed. Understood?"

The man was clearly conflicted, his eyes darting back and forth before his chest finally deflated. "Very well. But they don't leave until I have orders from an officer."

"Of course."

"What's going on here?"

Denys turned to see the captain of the King's Personal Guard rushing down the steps. Denys forced his most conciliatory face for the man, despite him not being of the aristocracy. "I am Sir Denys de Montfort, a member of the King's Court."

The captain bowed his head in appropriate respect. "I know who you are, Sir Denys. Did I hear you demand two dozen of my men?"

"You are aware that Lord Allard's daughter has been kidnapped?"

"I've heard she is missing, yes."

"Well, I have found her, and require men to back me up."

The captain frowned. "How many will we be facing?"

"At least a dozen, though how well trained they are, I cannot say."

The captain sighed. "I'm afraid I have none to spare. The King is in the country, and much of the guard is with him. I myself am only here for a few minutes to pass on urgent orders to the Court."

Denys leaned a little closer. "Do *you* want to be responsible for the death of Lord Allard's daughter? Do *you* want to answer to the King for her death, a death that *you* could have prevented?"

The man paled slightly as the implications played out in his mind, then he made a decision. "Very well. But I can only spare a dozen. Any more would risk the safety of the palace."

Denys decided it was best not to press his luck. A dozen armed, trained men, along with Marcus, Simon, and himself, should be enough to take on a dozen monks with questionable experience. "I'll take it."

Fingers were snapped, orders shouted, and within minutes, Denys was at the head of a column of armed men, charging through the gates and toward the unknown. A smile spread as the citizenry scrambled out of their way, fear and respect on their faces, reminding him of when he was younger, leading his men to war.

He missed those days.

Deeply sometimes.

Ahh, to be a soldier rather than an administrator.

Saint-Chapelle Church

Outskirts of Paris, Kingdom of France

Isabelle's heart hammered as the door opened and several monks entered. She stepped back toward the far wall, pressing against it, Annette leaning against her. The room was full now with all of the women who had been on the wagon with them. They were fed, bathed, and all wore simple dresses that didn't protect them much from the cold, though did display their assets a little too prominently for her liking. They were a bevy of beauties if there ever was one.

"It's time," said one of the monks, a smile on his face, his hood removed for the first time.

Her eyes narrowed, but she dared not ask what the monk who spoke was referring to.

"For what?" asked someone far braver, or stupider, than her.

The monk's smile broadened. "To return home."

Excited cries of relief erupted, and Isabelle hugged Annette as elation swept the room. The monk opened a door to the outside, holding out his hand, inviting them to follow. They all rushed out, the cold they were met with be damned. Isabelle gripped Annette's hand tightly, then shivered as she spotted the Lost Cause lurking behind, evil evident in the curl of her lip and the squint of her eyes.

Is she possessed again? Or is something else going on here?

Outside Saint-Chapelle Church
Outskirts of Paris, Kingdom of France

"Something's going on. The chanting has stopped."

Marcus chewed his cheek as he and his sergeant watched from behind a derelict building, barely half a wall left standing, though tall enough to shield them and their horses from anyone at the church.

"Here comes a wagon." Simon cursed as it rounded the far corner, evidently kept behind the church. "If that's not a horrid sight, I don't know what is."

Marcus had to agree, the wagon and its metal bars clearly a prison and not a means of comfortable transport. A priest emerged from the church, looking about as if satisfied with whatever had happened inside, a smile on his face.

"That has to be Mercier."

Marcus agreed. "I'll believe it for sure when I see—oh wait, there they are."

A dozen monks on horseback came from the back where their horses must have been hidden from the road along with the nightmarish cage on wheels. They took up position in front of and behind the wagon, confirming what they already knew.

Marcus gripped the hilt of his sword. "That's obviously him."

The priest climbed onto the carriage and flicked the reins, the entire procession underway within minutes.

Simon grunted. "They're not in a hurry."

Marcus nodded. "They obviously think nobody knows where they are. Isabelle and the others must be in the back of that wagon."

The procession had two ways to go, and Marcus held his breath to see which way they would come. And smiled as they turned their way.

Simon looked at him. "Just what are you smiling about?"

"They're coming this way."

Simon eyed him. "*Yes*, the *twelve* armed men are coming toward us *two* armed men."

Marcus mounted his horse. "We can't let them leave. Sir Denys may never find us if we follow, and we may never find them again if we don't."

"*Two* against *twelve*. Not exactly odds that are in our favor."

"We've faced worse."

Simon climbed into his saddle. "Have we? My memory isn't as good as yours."

Marcus thought back over their years together as he guided his horse from their hiding place. "Well, maybe not twelve. Ten?"

Simon growled. "I'm thinking six."

Marcus shook his head. "Definitely more than six." He frowned. "If only we had an archer. We could thin them out a bit."

Simon stared up at the heavens, his eyes closed, his lips moving. They stopped and he opened his eyes, peering out at the procession. He cursed.

"What?"

"My prayer wasn't answered."

Marcus laughed. "Then it is up to us to do God's work today."

Simon sighed. "Isn't it always?"

Marcus urged his horse forward. "Let's try not to die today, shall we?"

Simon shook his head. "I make no promises."

Leaving Saint-Chapelle Church
Outskirts of Paris, Kingdom of France

Father Mercier was exhausted, though content. They had saved a lot of souls today, and they would be delivered back to their families in short order. Today was their day of deliverance from evil, and he was responsible. He sighed, closing his eyes for a moment.

If only someone had been there to save Mother.

"Maintain your faith, and your mother will be saved."

He opened his eyes and looked at his constant companion, sitting beside him as they turned onto the road. "I know, but how many more must I save?" A hint of frustration made itself known, and he struggled to bury the un-Christian thought. He drew a deep breath. "I've saved so many, yet you say she is still condemned."

His companion smiled warmly at him, the look of understanding

214

and compassion washing over Mercier like a wave, and all his doubts were swept away. "Do not worry, I never ask of you more than you can manage. You know that."

Mercier nodded. He did know. Their forages into the wilds surrounding Paris almost always went smoothly, they always found those they were seeking, and they always managed to save the souls of those they found.

All except the Lost Cause, apparently already showing signs of reverting to her corrupted self.

With the exception of her, all had been successfully saved, and soon he would have another wagonful, and even more would be.

He flicked the reins, urging the horses on a little faster. "I know you don't, and I love my work. So much so that I would continue with it even if I knew my mother was saved." He glanced at his companion. "Surely, you must know that."

"I know, my son, I know. And you've said that before, but today, I believe you truly mean it."

Mercier caught his breath, his heart hammering. "Does-does that mean my mother has been saved?"

His companion put a hand on his shoulder. "Yes, my son, she has been."

Mercier's shoulders heaved with the lifting of the weight that had borne down on him for so many years. It was as if a chorus of angels were singing their welcome to his precious mother who had suffered so greatly for so long. A warmth spread from the hand on his shoulder and surged through his body, a rapturous bliss threatening to erupt from his chest. Tears streamed down his cheeks and he turned, finally gazing directly upon He who had guided him all these years.

"Thank you, my Lord."

And his savior blessed him with a smile, before pointing ahead. "Someone approaches, my son."

Mercier looked and frowned at the sight of two demons on horseback.

Outside Saint-Chapelle Church
Outskirts of Paris, Kingdom of France

Marcus brought his horse to a halt in the middle of a small bridge, blocking the procession, Simon to his right. He tossed his surcoat aside, revealing the hilt of his sword, but didn't draw it. Six of the monks on horseback advanced.

"Out of our way, Templar! We have no business with you."

Marcus leaned forward in his saddle, gesturing with his chin toward the priest, still seated. "But we have business with your master. Father Mercier, I believe his name is."

The mention of the name resulted in exchanged looks among those challenging them, and if Marcus could see their obscured faces clearly, he'd say they were nervous. It clearly meant that Father Brodeur had been right as to who was behind this, and confirmed that this was the group those that had left David for dead, had gone to meet.

But where are they?

They still only faced a dozen, which was how many David said he and Jeremy had encountered that first night. Could the others still be inside the church, preparing for the next ritual? It was possible. There had been no evidence that anyone had been in any hurry once the rituals had concluded.

But he was here for a reason. A specific reason. He rose in his saddle. "Isabelle, can you hear me? It's Marcus!"

He strained to listen for a reply, yet none came.

"Isabelle!" tried Simon, equally unsuccessful.

Marcus frowned, exchanging a confused glance with Simon. Could they have been wrong all along? Could Isabelle have never been with these men? But they knew Mercier was the one who had taken Isabelle, or at least he was fairly certain they did.

If only David were here. He could confirm that Mercier was the same priest that night.

No. He refused to believe there were two priests out there, scouring the countryside for the possessed, accompanied by a dozen armed monks. This had to be the right group, which meant that if Isabelle wasn't here, then they knew where she was.

Another possibility had him shuddering.

She could be dead.

He leaned over in his saddle, addressing the priest directly. "You are Father Mercier?"

"I am."

"Where is Isabelle? The girl you took in Crécy-la-Chapelle."

"The Isabelle you knew is dead," replied Mercier, rising. "The evil

218

that possessed her has been cleansed, demons, and if you do not let us pass, you too will be sent back to the darkness from which you came!"

Simon grunted. "Does he think we're demons?"

Marcus nodded. "I think so."

"He's insane."

Marcus frowned. "Which is what Father Brodeur said about him."

"Now what do we do?"

Marcus eyed their carefully chosen position. To pass, the monks would have to cross the narrow bridge they now occupied the other end of, which would limit them to no more than two riders at a time. They couldn't risk crossing the water, the ice liable to be too thin for the weight of the horses, which helped even the odds.

Unless they had archers, though Marcus continued to see no evidence of any.

As he watched the nervous energy on display, it was clear to him that these men were unaccustomed to being challenged. And why wouldn't they be? They were members of the clergy, doing the Lord's work, no matter how distasteful. Few would dare challenge anyone purporting to be with the Church.

Marcus gestured at the wagon. "I'm afraid we must insist on seeing our friend before we can let you go."

Mercier shook his head, sitting back down. "You were warned." He raised his hand then dropped it. "Dispatch them with haste. I want to make town by nightfall."

Simon muttered a curse as he drew his sword, Marcus suppressing the desire as he pulled his own. Two of the monks surged forward, toward the bridge, as they all drew their own swords. Marcus readied himself as his experienced eye took in everything around him. The way they held their swords, how they rode in the saddle, and what those behind the lead riders were doing. Was it organized? Coordinated? Or a muddled mess of those untrained in combat.

What he saw told him volumes, and it was that while some were inexperienced, too many showed they might prove worthy foes.

And they were all in the lead group.

Marcus raised his sword high and surged forward, his horse, supplied by the Templar Fortress, trained in battle and accustomed to what was about to happen. And the way his opponents were struggling to control their steeds in the tense situation suggested skittishness would be the order of their day.

It gave him and Simon a distinct advantage, though the odds were still twelve to two.

And that assumed no more came out of the church to help.

He dropped his sword hard, the blow parried easily by the monk he was matched with, but as they passed each other, Marcus drew a dagger with his left hand and swung backward in his saddle, the blade extended, and plunged it in the man's side, the ease at which the metal penetrated, confirming what Marcus had already suspected.

These men had no armor.

The monk cried out, gripping his side as Marcus yanked the blade free, urging his horse forward as he heard another cry, Simon finishing off the wounded man. With the knowledge nothing more than cloth protected those they faced, Marcus whipped the dagger at the second horseman, the blade embedding deeply in the man's chest. He slumped forward in his saddle, gripping at the hilt as he groaned in agony before slipping from his ride and falling over the edge of the bridge, breaking through the ice below.

With unfortunate consequences.

It revealed just how shallow the water was, and this revelation regrettably wasn't lost on those that remained. Four broke off, riding their horses through the water and up the embankment on the other side, opening up a second front, and cutting off any means of escape, Marcus and Simon now trapped on the bridge.

Simon grunted as he turned around to cover their rear. "Well, this is an unfortunate turn of events."

Marcus had to agree. "Do you want the six or the four?"

Simon's eyes widened. "I get a choice?"

Marcus smacked Simon's horse's hindquarters, sending it whinnying forward to face those that had crossed the disappointingly shallow water. "You take the four, old man!"

"Who are you calling old?"

Swords clashed behind him, and as long as he heard that, his sergeant was still alive, and four monks, two of whom he was confident had little experience from the way they held their swords, weren't much of a concern.

But the six?

Faced alone?

It could prove difficult. Though today was as good as any to die.

He raised his sword, yet to taste blood this cold afternoon, and charged.

Outskirts of Paris, Kingdom of France

David stopped Thomas with a hand. "Listen."

Thomas' eyes narrowed. "To what?"

David raised a finger, hissing for silence. "Do you hear that?"

Thomas shrugged, a little annoyed. "If I knew what I was supposed to be hearing, perhaps I could answer."

David continued to hold up a finger. "It sounds like swords clashing."

Thomas cocked an ear, cupping a hand around it, straining against the sounds of the occasional traveler, feet and hooves crunching on fresh snow making it difficult.

Then he heard it.

The distinctive sound of metal clashing against metal, the grunts and shouts of men in combat carrying over the snow-strewn landscape.

He opened his mouth to let David know, but the Templar squire was already racing forward, toward the fight. "Let's go! They could need help!"

Thomas followed at a distance, his riding skills lacking compared to the experienced Templar. As they raced toward the sound, a sound he had lost in the pounding of his horse on the road, he wondered what was expected of him should they find this fight. They were operating under the assumption that it was Sir Marcus, Sergeant Simon, and Sir Denys that were involved in some altercation, but what if it wasn't them? Would David insist on picking sides in a conflict they knew nothing about, or worse, perhaps force his way into the middle to stop the warring parties?

And would David expect him to be at his side?

Thomas had never been in anything beyond a bout of fisticuffs. Swords were metal sticks to him, and anyone with any experience would easily best him.

And what good would that do anybody?

He found himself slowing, the realization sending a wave of shame through him, his entire body numbing for a moment before he urged his horse forward. If it was Sir Marcus, then just the sight of two more men on their side could be enough to turn the tide of battle.

Thundering hooves behind him had him turning in his saddle. His eyes widened as he spotted Sir Denys, sword drawn, racing toward him, a dozen armed men on his heels.

"Move aside!" shouted Denys, apparently not recognizing him, and Thomas quickly complied. The gallant aristocrat, followed by a dozen of the King's finest, blew past him, and once clear, Thomas gave chase, his confidence that he might survive any altercation renewed.

We can't lose now!

Outside Saint-Chapelle Church
Outskirts of Paris, Kingdom of France

Marcus advanced, swinging his sword, the blow parried with ease, a counterblow swiftly delivered. He leaned back in his saddle, barely avoiding the tip of the blade, smiling at finally facing a worthy opponent.

"I see you have some experience, Monk."

His opponent flipped back his hood, revealing his face, their eyes finally meeting. "Ten years in the Holy Land, Templar. You'd be wise to surrender now, before you get hurt."

Marcus laughed as he swung his sword, maintaining his position on the bridge, preventing the others from helping their comrade. "Tell me, Monk, what is this priest's story? Why does he do what he does?"

Another swing, another parry.

"He does the Lord's work." His opponent grunted, delivering a forward jab with his blade. With a practiced signal to Marcus' horse with his knees, he avoided the blow with ease.

"But he isn't a priest. I know it, and I think you know it as well."

Another cry from behind had Marcus struggling to ignore the plight of his sergeant. As long as it wasn't a cry he was familiar with, and as long as the struggle continued, then his friend and comrade was still alive.

"Does the Church have sole discretion over all God's work?" asked his opponent as he swung. "Can a man who feels the love of God in his heart not perform His work?"

Marcus batted the blow to the side then shifted his sword's direction, catching the monk off guard, slicing into his right shoulder. "And is that what you do now? God's work? Attacking innocent men who simply want their friend released, a friend your priest claims to have saved the soul of? Why not just hand her over?"

The man switched hands, swinging his sword, barely any power behind the effort. Marcus caught the blade with his gloved hand, ending the fight. "Yield, or die."

The monk dropped his sword then gripped the wound oozing too much blood. He backed away and two more surged forward, leaving Marcus to shake his head. "Should I ask you the same question?"

They roared with forced bravado, Marcus confident his two new opponents were among the least experienced he had faced so far. He raised his sword when he noticed the priest had turned the wagon around and was heading away from the fight along with the man he had just wounded.

"The priest is leaving!"

Simon grunted behind him. "Good for bloody him. Is it too much to hope he's taking some of them with him?"

Marcus swung. "Unfortunately, only a wounded man." He reassessed the situation, stealing a quick glance over his shoulder to see Simon still faced two opponents. If Marcus were to break the line and go after the wagon, Simon would be left facing six alone, on both sides.

It was something he could never do to his friend.

One of the monks raised his sword to attack instead of parry, and Marcus' already swinging sword opened up the unwisely exposed midriff, which was one thing when equipped with chainmail as Marcus was, an entirely other thing when protected by a thin brown cloth. He fell to the ground, his companion rushing to replace him, his eyes wide with fear, when suddenly he groaned, falling forward in his saddle.

Marcus smiled at the arrow protruding from the man's back.

The next rider pulled on his reins, bringing his horse to a halt as he stared at the arrow in his comrade. Marcus sensed he was about to turn when an arrow pierced the man's throat, removing him from the battle, and substantially evening the odds.

"We have an archer on our side!"

Simon huffed. "Please tell him to direct an arrow or two in my favor, would you?"

Marcus laughed as he surged forward, not bothering to search for the source of the arrows. Whoever it was, was on their side, and that whoever was almost definitely David, one of the most skilled archers he had ever witnessed.

Another rider was felled, leaving Marcus facing a single opponent still blocking the road, the wagon in the distance, though well within sight. He was about to engage the man when the sound of pounding hooves to his left had him smiling at the sight of Sir Denys at the head of a column of the King's Personal Guard.

The final monk he was facing dropped his sword, raising his hands, and Marcus pointed at the wagon. "Stop him!"

Sir Denys nodded without saying anything, leading the charge, soon surrounding the wagon and bringing it to a halt.

Marcus was about to turn to help Simon when his friend bellowed at his opponents. "Where are you going? Don't you want to die today?"

He glanced over his shoulder to see the final two monks beating a hasty retreat. Marcus rose in his saddle. "Sir Denys!" Denys turned and Marcus pointed at the fleeing riders. Denys dispatched half a dozen of the guard to pursue, and Marcus indicated for his last opponent to head for the wagon as Denys' men raced past them on the bridge.

Marcus sheathed his sword as Simon came up beside him. "You okay?"

Simon thrust out his chest as he stretched. "I feel invigorated!"

"So, I should arrange for you to fight monks every day?"

Simon grinned. "If you could, it would be appreciated." Simon gave him the once over. "You appear none the worse for wear. I assume all that blood is theirs?"

Marcus glanced down at himself, smiling at the sight. "I assume so."

"And what was your favorite part of the battle?"

Marcus laughed. "I found the conversation stimulating." He motioned toward the wagon as they approached. "Let's go get Isabelle."

Simon grinned. "She is going to looove you for this."

Marcus rolled his eyes, though a small part of him began to worry. "Don't you dare start. Her heart belongs to Thomas."

Simon pointed ahead. "Speaking of."

Thomas rode up to the scene, a little out of breath, then stopped short of the wagon. Marcus beckoned him to join them, and the young man eyed the cage as he rode past the surrounded wagon, Father Mercier still sitting with the reins gripped in his hands. Marcus continued forward, closing the gap. He smiled at Thomas then waved at David as he spotted him several hundred paces to the right.

"I thought I told you two to go home."

Thomas shrugged. "David insisted, I'm afraid."

Marcus gripped the young man's shoulder, giving him a friendly shake. "I'm glad he did. You arrived just in time."

Thomas jerked a thumb at the King's men behind them. "I think they were more instrumental in your saving."

Simon spat. "We didn't need any saving. We had them exactly where we wanted them."

Marcus eyed his friend. "Surrounding us?"

"Exactly! Everyone was within reach of my sword."

Marcus shook his head, returning his attention to the wagon as the priest delivered a tirade aimed at Denys. It was a vitriolic display laced with colorful metaphors that should have shamed any member of the clergy for speaking them.

Thomas cleared his throat. "Umm, where's Isabelle?"

Marcus pointed toward the wagon. "You just passed her."

Thomas' eyes narrowed. "What do you mean?"

Marcus frowned. "I'd ask you the same thing."

Thomas pointed at the wagon. "If you're saying she's in there, then you're mistaken. It's empty."

Marcus leaped from his horse and ran over to the wagon, staring through the bars. And cursed. Thomas was right. No one was inside. He rounded the wagon and reached up, yanking the feet out from under the imposter priest. Mercier collapsed unceremoniously, and painfully, before Marcus grabbed him by the ankle and hauled him to the ground. He placed a foot squarely on the man's chest then applied pressure.

"Where are the women you took?"

Mercier glared up at him. "What business is it of yours, Demon? They've been saved, and are forever out of the reach of the evil you serve."

This man truly is mad.

Marcus pressed harder on the man's chest. "Where are they?"

"Where you can never find them!"

Marcus stared down the road toward the church where Mercier had been carrying out his rituals. "They must still be at the church!" He mounted his horse, brought forward by Simon, and they both charged toward the church in the distance. It had been almost half an hour since they had spotted them leaving, and Marcus feared the worst.

If Isabelle and the others had left at the same time as Mercier and his men, but in the opposite direction, they could be anywhere by now.

And lost to them forever if that anywhere was Paris.

Paris, Kingdom of France

"Where are we going?" asked Isabelle, no fear in her heart now. The carriage they were in was magnificent, unlike anything she had ever experienced as a farm girl, and they were all in good spirits despite there being a couple too many crammed inside. But none of that mattered to her as she stared out the window revealing a bright, beautiful day, and the fascinating streets of Paris.

And more important than the sights, was the fact there were no locks, no chains, no guards, just the women who had been "saved," and two monks, now in civilian attire, sitting up front. One of them replied.

"To a benefactor's house. There you'll get a proper meal and some bedrest, then you'll be returned to your homes tomorrow."

The response was cheery, these men who were once their captors, now evidently their friends. Isabelle sighed, squeezing Annette's hand, eliciting a smile from her friend. "Didn't you say you were from Paris?"

Annette nodded. "Yes. Perhaps I can see my family tonight, though it would be nice to be presentable before doing so." She gripped Isabelle's hand in both of hers. "Isn't it so exciting!"

Isabelle smiled. "We'll definitely have a story to tell, though I'm still not sure exactly what happened."

"Best you keep that to yourself."

Smiles were wiped from every face as they turned to the chilling voice of the Lost Cause.

"Why?" asked Isabelle.

"Talk of it might bring back the demons." She stared at each of them then burst into a spinetingling cackle that had them all shuffling away from her as best they could.

"We're here!" announced one of their escorts.

The uneasiness was forgotten as everyone tried to get a look at their benefactor's home. Isabelle's eyes widened as they passed through a set of gates that closed behind them before they stopped in front of a grand set of steps leading to a set of massive, wooden doors. They were helped out of the carriage by their escorts, then led up the steps and through the doors, revealing an interior unlike anything Isabelle had ever experienced.

"It's bigger than our church!" she gushed. "Is this normal in Paris?"

Even Annette seemed impressed. "No, this is something rather special. Even my father's estate isn't this extravagant."

Isabelle's eyes roamed the entire structure, her eyes narrowing. "Where are the beds? The kitchen?"

Annette giggled, patting her on the hand. "This is merely the grand foyer. There are probably dozens if not scores of other rooms here." She pointed to a wide staircase. "There's at least one other floor."

Isabelle shook her head at the opulence, unable to fathom why anyone would need a home so large, then pointed at the floor, a black and white checkered pattern extending to all four corners, and so shiny, she could almost see her face.

A set of gold gilded doors opened in front of them and a group of men, dressed as none she had ever seen, stepped through, led by a man in long, red, flowing robes. Their escorts quickly arranged the women into a row, then bowed.

Isabelle executed an awkward curtsey along with the others.

The man in red smiled, holding out his hands. "Welcome, my children, welcome. I hope you are all well today?"

Murmured replies were offered, and Isabelle watched curiously as the man went to the end of the line to her left, where the Lost Cause stood. He was clearly in charge, based upon the deference shown him, which meant he must be their benefactor.

The man tsked, shaking his head, his expression one of sorrow. "How are you feeling today, my dear?"

She shrugged. "Like I'm living on the edge."

He sighed. "That's unfortunate." He took her hand and patted it. "One of these days, one of these days." He reached up and ran the back of his finger against her cheek. A flash of a smile was exchanged at the touch, and if Isabelle didn't know better, it suggested an understanding between the two of something more than their brief exchange was meant to reveal.

He moved on to Annette, taking her chin between his thumb and forefinger, moving her head about as he examined her from all angles.

"Beautiful girl, very beautiful."

"I'm the daughter of—"

The man cut her off with a raised finger. "Here, you only speak when spoken to."

The delivery was curt and final, and Annette's jaw snapped shut as she exchanged a confused look with Isabelle, who now found herself under the man's uncomfortable gaze.

"Now, *you* truly are an uncommon beauty." He reached out for her face and she recoiled. "She has spirit, this one." His hand darted out and he caught her chin, gripping in tightly, painfully. "We'll soon cure you of that affliction."

He stepped back, moving to the next in line, and she suppressed a gasp as she finally noticed the large gold cross around his neck, his odd robes suddenly reminding her of some of the clergy she had seen in her life. This man was clearly associated with the Church, yet he was sizing them up like meat at a market.

It made no sense.

And what did he mean they would cure her? That implied time, and they had been told they would be leaving the next day for home.

On a foolish impulse, she stepped forward. "What is going on here?"

The man turned back toward her, a bemused expression on his face. "My child, did you not hear me say that you only speak when spoken to?"

Isabelle was certain something was wrong, and she could imagine nothing worse than what she had already been through. Annette reached out, grabbing her arm, trying to haul her back into line. Isabelle wrenched her arm loose. "No, I want to know what is happening. We were told we were being taken home."

The man smiled. "But my child, you are mistaken. *This* is your new home."

Isabelle felt faint, and her knees almost gave out. "Wh-what do you mean?"

The man in red stepped closer. He grabbed her by the waist and pulled her tight against his body, something unpriestly pressing against her thigh, his breath hot on her face as he leaned in. "This, my dear, is Babylon. Here, you will serve the needs of the rich, of the powerful, of your betters. Here, you will fulfill the desires of those whose demands are of a particular nature. Here, you will do as you are told, when you are told, or face consequences far more terrible than you can possibly imagine." His hand gripped her behind and she gasped. "Do you understand me?"

She did.

And she didn't.

Her mind was far too simple, her life experiences far too limited, to truly understand what he meant.

But she had been right about one thing.

Something was wrong, and it was far worse than she had feared.

Here, she, like the others, was merely a piece of meat, to be consumed by those who were far more important than simple farm girls plucked from the countryside merely because they were beautiful.

It had all been a ruse.

None of them were possessed.

Everything was a lie.

She stared at the Lost Cause, and the smile told Isabelle everything she needed to know.

The Lost Cause was part of it, the bait laid out for the simple villagers to take, terrifying their naïve minds with her antics into thinking that what the priest said was true, convincing them to give up their children and loved ones for saving.

But why the ritual? Why had the priest bothered with that? Was he innocent in all this?

Yet none of it mattered now. She was here, and no one knew where she was. She had been condemned to a life of horrors she couldn't possibly imagine, yet she feared she would learn all too soon.

Why, Lord, are you letting this happen?

The world spun, and within moments, she slid down the body of the man in red, collapsing to the floor, her will to live gone.

Saint-Chapelle Church

Outskirts of Paris, Kingdom of France

The church was empty. Evidence of whatever ritual had happened here earlier still remained, and a back room suggested the women had been taken there and stripped then washed before leaving. It was a disturbing sight, and Marcus' heart ached for their friend Isabelle and what she must have gone through.

Simon pointed at a set of clothing sitting on the floor next to other bundles. "Isn't that Isabelle's?"

Marcus had no idea, but a trembling Thomas nodded. "Yes. I brought it for her the last time I visited." He collapsed onto a nearby bench, grabbing his hair as he rocked back and forth. "We're never going to find her."

Marcus exchanged a frown with Simon. He wanted to say something encouraging, something to boost the young man's spirits, yet what that could be beyond platitudes escaped him. Instead, he placed a hand on Thomas' shoulder for a moment and gave it a gentle squeeze.

Sir Denys walked in from outside, shaking his head. "We lost the tracks not a couple of hundred paces from here. The roads are just too busy now. They appear to have been heading for the city, however."

"See!" cried Thomas before returning to his hair pulling.

Marcus understood his despair, and shared it. If they had headed out of the city, there might have been a chance of splitting up and taking every possible route, and should the good Lord have granted it, a miracle might have taken place. But the city? There was no hope of finding them without a destination.

Thomas rose and picked up Isabelle's clothes, holding them tight against him and smelling the soiled garments as if trying to find a piece of her to cling to. The pathetic sight enraged Marcus and he growled, a decision made.

"We have to make the priest talk." He stormed from the room and back into the nave, marching toward Mercier and the surviving monks, all held by the King's Personal Guard. "Where did you take them?"

Mercier stared up at him. "Like I said, Demon, where you can never find them again."

Marcus glared at him. "But I thought they were going home."

Mercier regarded him for a moment. "They are where they will be loved and where your master can't find them again."

Marcus' eyes narrowed. "What are you talking about?" He turned to the monks. "He's mad, isn't he?"

Nobody replied, though it was clear to him by their awkward looks they agreed.

But one had a slight smirk.

Marcus drew his sword and pressed it against the chest of the smirker. "Speak or die."

The man stared up at him, the smirk gone, fear in his eyes. "I can't say anything."

Marcus pressed a little harder, the man gulping as he stared down at the blade. "Why? Loyalty to this false priest?" Marcus leaned closer. "You do know that, right? That he's not a priest?"

The man nodded and Marcus smiled. On the inside.

Now let's hope that's the first of many answers.

He looked at the others. "You all know this?"

Nods all around.

"I *am* a priest!" cried Mercier. "The Lord himself is at my side during all my efforts. Would He do so should I not be a member of the clergy?"

"I've spoken with Cardinal Nicolas and Father Brodeur, your former instructor at the University, and I've been assured that you are *not* an ordained priest. In fact, you were kicked out of the University."

Mercier spit on the ground. "Never mention the Cardinal's name in my presence again. No matter how many times I begged him to help me in my quest, he would turn me away."

"Your quest?"

"All women of uncommon beauty are the work of the Devil, and must have their souls cleansed so they can lead good, productive lives." He growled. "The Cardinal didn't agree with me. He never did. He said I was mad, just as you say here today. But I'm not, I tell you!" He looked to his left. "Yes, my Lord, I'll tell him." He turned back to Marcus, who exchanged a confused glance with the others.

Does he really think the Lord is actually at his side?

"It was these brave men"—Mercier pointed at the monks—"that came to me with the poor creature we now call the Lost Cause. I tried to save her, but failed, but they too recognized the evil existing among us, and offered to join me in my quest. And thanks to them, we have saved scores over the past several years."

Scores?

A pit formed in Marcus' stomach. "What have you done with these women?"

"I've freed them of the evil that possessed them. My faithful servants are returning them home as we speak."

Marcus stared at the man. He was clearly insane. He apparently thought Jesus himself guided him, and if he felt that way, then he must truly believe he was doing good. The church had been set up for a ritual of some type, and there was a rear room where it appeared the abducted women had been fed and given an opportunity to clean themselves. The clothes left behind suggested they had been given clean ones. None of that implied any ill will after the ritual.

He stepped closer to the priest, forcing a gentler tone. "After the ritual, do *you* see them again?"

Mercier's shoulders slumped as he sighed heavily. "Only the Lost Cause. That poor one continually gets repossessed." He looked up at Marcus. "It happens. The evil she had been cursed with is sometimes too strong even for me. But this time, the Lord Himself told me that she would soon be forever freed, and thanks to the untiring efforts of myself and my loyal men, the condemned soul of my beloved mother has been saved, and she has been granted entry into the Kingdom of Heaven."

Marcus stepped away, scratching his chin as Simon and Denys huddled with him in the corner.

"What do you think?" asked Denys, eyeing the man over Marcus' shoulder.

"I think he's mad, but I think he believes he truly is doing good."

Simon scowled. "So, you think he's telling the truth about the women being returned?"

Marcus shook his head. "I don't know. Something is going on. Why would the monks fight us? Why not just let us look in their wagon, then tell us where the women had been taken?"

Simon inhaled deeply through his nose as he stared at the men they had fought. "Loyalty? Remember, it wasn't the monks that started the fight, it was Mercier who ordered them to."

Marcus nodded. His sergeant was right, though blind loyalty didn't fit here. "But they know he's mad. They've all admitted it."

Simon chewed his cheek. "The one you questioned seemed scared, and I got the impression it wasn't the priest he was scared of."

"Agreed." Marcus glanced over his shoulder at the monks. "I think they're the key to finding Isabelle and the others, not Mercier. I think he's quite mad and truly believes the women have returned home."

Denys lowered his voice. "You think these men are using him? What did he say? That he met with the Cardinal, then these men found him? Could the Cardinal have sent them?"

Marcus' eyes narrowed as his chest tightened with the disturbing suggestion. "But why? Why would the Cardinal do that?"

Denys shook his head. "I have no idea, but the monks, or whatever they are, are the key to finding your friend. I think we should focus on them."

Marcus agreed. "We'll separate them. Get each one away from their friends then interrogate them."

The corner of Simon's lip curled. "Roughly, if necessary."

The sound of horses arriving outside had them turning to the doors as they swung open, revealing the new arrivals, their manner of dress suggesting they were from the King's Court.

"Who is in charge here?"

Sir Denys cleared his throat. "That would be me."

The man turned to him. "By order of the King's Court, at the behest of Cardinal Nicolas, these prisoners are to be transferred into our custody immediately, and you and any outside parties"—he eyed Marcus and Simon for a moment with disdain—"are to have no further contact with them."

Marcus was about to challenge them when Denys placed the back of his hand on the Templar Knight's chest. "There is the matter of the women that are still missing," said Denys in as level a tone as Marcus was sure the man could muster.

The Court's representative seemed caught off guard. "What women?"

Denys put on an exaggerated expression and tone. "The women these men have been taking all across the countryside, of course!"

The man paused, then shook his head. "I know nothing of that." He turned to Mercier. "What of it, Father? Where are these women?"

"On their way home, as I've been trying to tell these servants of the Devil."

The man turned back to Denys. "There you have it. Surely a member of the clergy wouldn't lie."

Denys lost control, stabbing a finger at Mercier. "But the man is insane! He's not even a priest!"

"I am so!"

It was Marcus' turn to offer a steadying hand. "There's no point. He has his orders, and there will be no reasoning with him." His eyes narrowed. "But how did they find out we were here?"

Denys cursed, turning his back to the Court officials. "I'm afraid that's my fault. I sent one of the men to inform the Court of the situation, and to expect the arrival of prisoners. I never imagined an order like this would be given."

"They're taking them," muttered Simon.

They all turned to watch Mercier and the monks as they were led outside, and Marcus took a slight bit of satisfaction in seeing them loaded into the back of their own wagon of horrors. He hoped it suggested justice might prevail, though he had his doubts.

"What do we do now?" asked Thomas. "We have to find Isabelle, and the only hope of that is in the back of that wagon!"

Simon put a hand on the young man's shoulder. "And we're forbidden from any contact. This is ridiculous!"

Marcus nodded, in full agreement with his friends. Then something occurred to him. "Remember who made that demand?"

Simon stared at him. "The Cardinal?"

"Exactly. Why would the Cardinal want to stop us?"

Denys shook his head. "I'm afraid it could be as simple as you, a Templar, being involved. After our initial meeting with him, it was quite evident he hated you and your order vehemently."

Marcus frowned. "Could it be as petty as that?"

Denys sighed. "In Paris, I'm afraid, many questionable things can be boiled down to petty jealousies."

"But what do we do?" cried an exasperated Thomas, his eyes filled with tears. "We have to do something!"

Marcus regarded the young man for a moment, at a loss for any comforting words. Denys saved him.

"I suggest we all return home, and I will immediately petition the Court for access to the prisoners." He shrugged. "It's all I can think of to do."

Marcus clenched his teeth in frustration as he watched the wagon pull away, along with all the guardsmen that had joined them in the fight.

"And what if they don't give us access?" asked Thomas.

Marcus squared his shoulders as he stared out the open doors at the mass of depravity in the distance. "Then we'll tear this city apart until we find her."

Babylon

Paris, Kingdom of France

Isabelle trembled in the corner of the bed of what she feared might be her new permanent home. The room was a good size, about half the size of her humble home in Crécy-la-Chapelle, but with no windows, and a door that locked from the outside. It was well appointed, and as beautiful as any room she had ever seen. In fact, if she weren't so terrified, she might have enjoyed exploring it.

Instead, she sat, her knees drawn up to her chest, her arms wrapped around them, as she rocked back and forth, her tears long dried up, shock setting in. She stared at herself in the mirror on the opposite wall, something she had never done before.

She *was* beautiful.

She had to admit it, though it felt vain. And from what the man in red had said, she was certain that's why she was here. It had nothing to do with demonic possession or any other such nonsense, though she was quite certain Father Mercier had thought it was. It was clear to her now that the monks were behind everything. It was them that had told her to pretend to be possessed. The only reason she could think of for them to say that, was to fool Mercier.

Were they using the man for their own ends? All of the women were beautiful, and that reason was used to take some of the women she had witnessed torn from their own communities. And now, here she was, in some sort of palatial estate, told she would "service" those that were better than her.

And she knew what that meant.

Carnal relations.

She was to be a sexual partner for men. She had heard of such things, though had never imagined them to be true. And the stories she had heard were always of whores in the back alleys of Paris, or houses of ill repute where the filth of society congregated for all manners of interactions. But this place? It seemed fit for a king. She would never have imagined that people so rich would have need of such services.

She hugged her knees tighter, trembling at the thought of what was to come. She had never experienced being with a man. She had kissed Thomas, and had wondered what it would be like to go further, but she would never give herself over before marriage.

Oh, Thomas! Where are you?

The sound of a key turning in the lock had her, for a brief moment, idiotically thinking her prayers had been answered. Instead, two plainly dressed women entered, then another followed, matronly in appearance, with a demeanor of one who never tolerated being talked back to.

"Your name?" she demanded curtly.

"I-Isabelle."

"Stand when you're spoken to!"

Isabelle flinched then scrambled to her feet, pressing against the wall farthest from the new arrivals.

"I am Mrs. Prudhomme, and I'm here to make a lady of you."

Isabelle's eyes narrowed, this rather unexpected. "Wh-why?"

"So that you may entertain your patrons. Those who frequent this place are of the finest breeding, and they expect the companions we provide to at least pretend to be of similar station. The better you do, the better the experience you will have. Should you resist your training, you will be relegated to the chambers below, where you will service the less, shall we say, discerning clientele of this establishment."

Isabelle's heart pounded as she listened, not sure of what to make of everything. She simply couldn't fathom what this place was, whom these patrons could be, or why such polite and innocuous terms were being used. Wasn't this a house of ill repute, where whores served the scum of society? Yet none of what Mrs. Prudhomme said seemed to indicate that, yet Isabelle knew it did.

Her shoulders slumped in defeat. "Wh-what is this place?"

"None of your concern. All you need to know is that only the most discerning gentlemen come here to have their every desire satisfied. And should you make them happy, you too will have a wonderfully comfortable life, filled with fine clothes, food, perfumes, and even jewelry." Prudhomme stepped closer, her expression stern. "But should you disappoint, it will be to the chambers for you, until you can take it no more. Understood?"

It wasn't. None of it was, though she felt a nod was the appropriate response.

A smile flashed. "Good. Time to clean you up." The woman clapped twice. "Ladies!"

The other two advanced, and Isabelle cried out as the most humiliating experience of her life began.

Durant Residence

Paris, Kingdom of France

Jeremy spotted Thomas' house ahead and sighed with relief. He was as near death as he had ever been, he was certain, most of the feeling in his body forgotten, sheer will the only reason he had made it here. He managed to roll out of his saddle and onto the snow-covered ground, then hitch his horse, Tanya staring up at him, panting with concern.

He knocked on the door, the knocks weak, and he feared for a moment he might not have been heard. He could barely raise his head to see who opened it a moment later.

"Jeremy!" cried Thomas, answering his question. "Come in!"

Jeremy shuffled inside as Tanya bolted past him, and he closed his eyes, almost crying at the sound of Sir Marcus, Simon, and David greeting the dog.

"Tanya, I thought I left you at home!" said David as Jeremy

collapsed in Thomas' arms, the last ounce of strength drained from him.

Thomas dragged him toward the fire, stretching Jeremy's broken ribs, and he cried out before fainting momentarily. He could hear the concerned shouts of his master and sergeant in the distance, then the faint sensations of multiple hands on him as he was carried carefully in front of the fire. His clothes were quickly stripped off him, and as the warmth radiated out from the roaring flames, he felt the life get pushed back into his body.

"It looks like he's broken his ribs," said Simon.

"But he was treated by someone. There's no way he could have wrapped himself like this," said Marcus, the voices getting closer now.

He smiled slightly at the next voice, that of his best friend David. "I'll remove these and check the wound." He felt some tugging at his chest, then a few moments later, the sweet relief of his lungs finally expanding and taking in a full breath, even if it was excruciating. "I'll rewrap him—"

"No."

David's voice got louder. "Jeremy, can you hear me?"

"Yes."

"Can you open your eyes?"

Jeremy struggled, but finally managed, finding himself surrounded by the concerned looks of Marcus, Simon, David, Thomas, and one curious mastiff. "I-I made it."

Marcus frowned. "Barely, by the looks of it." He pointed at David. "Go to the Fortress and get a nurse. Also let them know we found him."

"Yes, sir." David patted Jeremy on the shoulder, flashing him a smile, then disappeared from sight, the door opening a few minutes later with a gust that reminded Jeremy how cold it was outside.

"Thomas, get him some of that tisane to warm him."

Thomas disappeared, reappearing a few moments later with a steaming cup. Simon helped Jeremy to a sitting position, placing himself behind him and acting as the back of a chair, taking the cup from Thomas and pressing it to Jeremy's lips.

"Open your mouth, you fool."

Jeremy parted his lips slightly and felt the hot liquid pour into his mouth, thawing his tongue and cheeks. He swallowed, the act difficult, but with each sip, he could feel the warmth spread through his insides, and it was wonderful.

Marcus turned to Thomas. "Ask a favor of our new friends, the Carons. Tell them we need a hearty soup as quickly as possible."

Thomas nodded, heading out the door moments later. Jeremy continued to sip the tisane as the warmth from the fire worked its magic. The tingling in his fingers and toes was almost unbearable, but after a few minutes, it faded, and he could once again wiggle them.

"Give me a moment," he said, reaching up and pushing the cup away. He sat up with his own strength, gasping and grabbing at his ribs. "I-I need to lie down." He stretched out, facing the fire, his hand gripping his side. Simon put the cup on the floor in front of him. "Thanks."

Marcus sat across from him, cross-legged on the floor. "Can you talk?"

"I-I think so." He took another sip of his tisane. "It's these ribs, they're agony. Every breath I take, every move I make." He winced.

"It's torture."

Marcus agreed. "I've broken some ribs in my time. What happened? We thought you were dead."

A lump formed in Jeremy's throat as shame washed over him. He closed his burning eyes. "I lost her. I'm sorry, but they figured out they were being followed because I did something foolish. They ambushed me." He gently patted his ribs. "I took a sword to the side. Fortunately, my chainmail saved me." He groaned. "Though I think death would have been less painful." He stared up at Marcus, regret consuming him. "I lost them in a storm." He dropped his gaze. "I failed you."

Marcus grunted. "Nonsense. And we found the priest and his so-called monks."

Jeremy brightened, a hopeful smile spreading as his eyes opened wide. "Then you have Isabelle?" He looked over his shoulder, ignoring the roar of pain, searching for her. "Where is she?"

"I'm afraid she and the others were already gone by the time we captured the priest."

"Where?"

"They claim home, but we fear the worst. Sir Denys is trying to get permission to interrogate the monks."

Jeremy lay his head back down. "I don't understand. I thought you captured them."

"We did, but men from the Court came and took the prisoners under orders from the Cardinal."

Jeremy's eyes narrowed. "The Cardinal? Why would he be involved."

"We're not sure."

The door opened and Thomas rushed in with two of the neighbors, carrying a large pot between them. Marcus rose with a smile.

"That was quick."

Thomas shrugged. "They're offering us their dinner. I tried to refuse, but they wouldn't listen."

"We can cook another, not to worry." The woman spotted Jeremy on the floor. "My word, what happened to you?"

"My first French winter," replied Jeremy.

The two women rushed forward and Thomas closed the door. Food was soon being shoveled into Jeremy's mouth by one, the other marshaling hot water and cloths, beginning to bathe him from head to embarrassing toe.

"Remind me to get broadsided next time," muttered Simon.

"Remember your vows," chuckled Marcus.

"Hey, get out of there!"

Everyone turned to see Thomas pulling Tanya off a pile of clothes sitting on the table.

"Leave those alone!" he cried. "They might be all I have left of her!"

Jeremy gasped as something down below was washed.

"Don't worry, love, it's nothing I haven't seen before. I've got four boys, you know."

"And a husband who likes to be washed down there!"

The two roared with laughter as Jeremy closed his eyes, praying to God for deliverance from this humiliation.

"Why is Tanya with you?"

Jeremy dared not look at his master while the work below continued and biology took over. "Umm, she found me somehow. I was nearly frozen to death in an abandoned barn, and she was there when I woke up, or more accurately, when *she* woke me up. She saved my life."

Simon grunted. "Quite the nose on her."

"Indeed," agreed Marcus. "Are you thinking what I'm thinking?"

The job below done, his vows barely intact, Jeremy opened his eyes and looked up at Sir Marcus, a smile on his master's face as he stared at Tanya.

Simon grunted. "I've learned to just say no."

Outskirts of Paris, Kingdom of France

They had left David with Jeremy, despite both their protests. Jeremy was in no condition to join them, despite the guilt that tortured him, and somebody had to stay with him. Thomas' insistence on coming with them once he had learned of Marcus' idea, had made the decision easy through process of elimination.

And Marcus had to admit, his idea was working brilliantly.

So far.

When Tanya had sniffed Isabelle's clothes, it occurred to him that it had to be because she recognized the smell, and then he had remembered David's surprise at the dog being there. And that had begged the question, why *was* the dog there? Jeremy's answer had provided them, hopefully, with the solution to finding Isabelle.

After returning to the abandoned church, Tanya had little trouble picking up Isabelle's scent, and had them inside the city in no time.

Unfortunately, it was almost nightfall, and it was becoming difficult to travel quickly, though that wasn't a problem for Tanya, who had to continually be called to slow down, as galloping horses through the streets of Paris was a dangerous proposition, especially for the innocent on foot.

It was soon clear they were heading for the finer section of the city, and when Tanya made a beeline for a rather large estate, Marcus ordered her back and dismounted.

"Is this the place, girl?"

Tanya barked, straining to continue her hunt.

"Stay," ordered Marcus, pointing at the ground. Tanya sat, panting in expectation of her next order. Marcus and the others surveyed the estate that lay ahead of them. It was well lit, and the gates were opening and closing as horse-drawn carriages of the finest quality appeared every few minutes, the coachman of each handing over a scroll of some sort to one of those on guard, then once inspected, they were let through, those inside the carriages never disturbed.

"Notice anything about those carriages?"

Simon shrugged. "Should I?"

"None of them have any markings. No family crests."

Simon grunted. "Interesting. So, if they are spotted going in, nobody knows who they are."

"Exactly."

"But these are clearly wealthy people. Why go to such trouble?"

Marcus pursed his lips. "If I had to guess, it would be because whatever is happening on the other side of those walls, would be frowned upon by much of society."

"What do you think is going on?" asked Thomas, trepidation in his voice.

Marcus sighed. "I fear to say it, lest it becomes true, but think about it. Nothing but beautiful women were taken by the priest, then the monks supposedly return them to their homes. Now, Tanya leads us here." His jaw clenched. "I think these beautiful women *never* return home. I think they all end up here, to be used by these men that arrive in their anonymous carriages."

Simon growled. "If any of them lay a hand on Isabelle, I'll dispatch them to Hell myself."

"So, what do we do?" asked Thomas. "Surely this place is well-guarded."

Marcus stared at the gates, and the little bit he could see beyond. "Perhaps, though perhaps not. I see only four on the gate, but nothing beyond. And those four are dressed more as servants, not guards."

"Seems rather foolish," observed Simon.

"Not necessarily. Remember, what trouble might they really expect here? This is Paris' finest, not the riffraff one might normally expect at a house of ill repute."

Simon grabbed the hilt of his sword. "I say we overwhelm those at the gate, storm inside, demand they hand over Isabelle, then leave."

Marcus frowned. "And what of the other women?"

Simon eyed him. "Okay, we overwhelm those at the gate, storm inside, demand they hand over Isabelle *and* the other women, then leave."

Marcus chuckled. "No, I'm sure there are enough men there to cause us more than an inconvenience. We need manpower."

Simon's eyes narrowed. "Who? Our brothers?"

Marcus shook his head. "No, if the aristocracy is somehow involved, that could only cause trouble for our order."

Simon grunted. "Well, the King's Personal Guard is out of the question, if recent events are any indication." He gave Marcus a look. "Why am I bothering? You already have the answer, don't you?"

Marcus grinned. "Don't I always."

Simon bowed with a flourish. "Yes, you do, my master. Would you bless us with your wisdom?"

Marcus laughed. "Lord Allard has a substantial personal guard, and Sir Denys has at least half a dozen at his command. Together, they should be enough to overwhelm any guard here and secure the release of the women." He mounted his horse. "You and Thomas go to Sir Denys and bring every man he can spare here. I'll go to Lord Allard and gather his men. We'll meet back here as soon as possible."

Babylon

Paris, Kingdom of France

Marcus was content to let a very determined Lord Allard led the procession, three dozen men on horseback, fully armed, even if some were only stable boys. They approached the gate of the estate they suspected was holding Isabelle, Lord Allard's daughter Annette, and the others. The four guards appeared confused, and one ran for the main house.

"Open this gate in the name of the King!" demanded Allard, his presence commanding, as impressive as any Marcus had seen in battle.

The one evidently in charge of this post stepped forward, hesitantly. "I'm sorry, m'Lord, but no one enters Babylon without a pass."

Allard's eyes narrowed. "Babylon? What is this place?"

"I'm afraid I cannot say." He held out a hand, directing them away from the estate. "I'm afraid I must ask you to move along."

Allard roared, drawing his sword and swinging, the blade burying itself halfway through the man's neck before it came to a stop. He kicked out with his boot, pushing the corpse off the blade, then advanced on the remaining guards. "Do I repeat myself?"

The gates were pulled open and the two remaining guards bolted into the night, Allard already pushing forward. Marcus turned to Sir Denys. "Leave four men to guard the gate. No one gets in or out."

Denys nodded, executing the orders, the gates slamming shut behind them. Allard led the charge to the main entrance of the impressive estate, shouts of warning going up from inside, a stream of armed guards rushing out moments later in response.

Though it wouldn't be enough.

To their left, there was a row of carriages and a group of coachmen milling about, now staring at the new arrivals, their mouths agape. Allard charged his horse up the wide steps, swinging his sword, Marcus and Simon flanking him, helping dispatch the ill-prepared and poorly trained guards.

Clearly no one had ever expected such an occurrence. Screams from both men and women greeted them as the din of the attack reached those inside, the warning shouts continuing as the word spread. The doors slammed shut and Marcus dismounted, rushing up to them and throwing his shoulder into one of the two large wooden barriers. It gave slightly, though held.

But it gave.

He motioned to the others to work the door as he stepped back. A carriage began its escape, and Marcus noticed a door open at the far left of the estate, one he hadn't spotted before. Men were piling out, in various states of dress, struggling into their respective carriages. He was prepared to ignore them, as they would be stopped at the gates by Sir Denys' men, when he paused, the first of the carriages heading to the rear of the estate instead.

"There's a rear gate!"

Allard turned, spotting the escaping carriages, then pointed at some of his men. "Stop them!"

"Yes, m'Lord!" A dozen of his guard, still on horseback, gave chase as a cry of triumph erupted from the men at the door as it finally splintered then gave.

Marcus, with Simon at his side, surged forward and into the estate, the men spreading out through the grand entranceway, the opulence on display enough to rival the King's own court. Servants were scrambling out of the way, hugging the walls or trying to find some means of escape.

Marcus grabbed one of them. "Where are the women?"

The man pointed a shaky finger to the left, and Marcus rushed toward a set of wooden doors, intricately carved, and threw them open. Shocked screams met him and the others, dozens of women inside, dressed in the finest of clothes, their hairs in styles he had rarely seen. All were beautiful, and all, from any outward appearance, willingly there.

"Isabelle! Are you here?"

Allard rushed up beside him. "Annette, darling, are you here?"

There was no response. One of the women tentatively rose from a couch filled with cushions, and warily approached.

"Are-are you here to save us?"

None appeared to be in need of it, but Marcus nodded. "If you require it, then yes."

She collapsed in his arms, sobbing, her shoulders heaving as she thanked him profusely. "I'm from Châtres. They took me two years ago. Can you take me home to my papa?"

Marcus watched, his mouth agape, his heart aching at the sight, as the dozens of women rushed toward their saviors, some crying, some overjoyed, and all hugging them, desperate to tell their stories, stories that hadn't been heard by anyone, for there had never been anyone willing to listen.

He gently pushed the woman in his arms away. "Are there others?"

"Yes. There are rooms upstairs." She shivered. "And rooms downstairs. The chambers."

Tanya barked behind them and Marcus turned to see Thomas, who had been told to remain outside with the mastiff until called for, chasing after the dog, up the stairs. Marcus and Simon took after them, and as they reached the second floor, they found several hallways, Tanya sprinting down one of them. They gave chase and found her near the end, scratching at a door, whimpering.

Marcus hammered on the door. "Isabelle! Are you in there?"

"Oh God, yes! Yes, I am!"

Relief swept over Marcus as he tried the door. It was locked. He stepped back, kicking it open, and before he could enter, a bundle of hair and tears rushed into his arms.

"Oh, thank God you're here! I thought I would be trapped here forever!"

Marcus gently pushed her away then nodded toward Thomas, who stood several paces away, awaiting his turn.

"Thomas!" She threw herself into his arms and the young man

hugged her hard. "I swear, no one touched me, I swear it. I'm still worthy, I promise you!"

Marcus' eyes burned and his chest ached at the poor girl's pleadings. That her first words to the man she loved would be to try and assure him that she hadn't been defiled, was heartbreaking, and it enraged him as he stared at the dozens of doors lining the walls.

He stepped away to give them some privacy, and he and Simon, soon joined by others, began opening the doors. Some of the rooms proved empty, but too many, far too many, were occupied by terrified, imprisoned women, their nightmarish stories crushing his spirit. Though it was those that merely responded with blank stares, with no emotion, the broken souls of months or years of abuse, that had him near tears. He had seen that look before, and he feared they would never be the same.

Never.

"Annette!"

"Papa!"

A young woman bolted past them and into the arms of Lord Allard, the tearful reunion bringing a smile to Marcus' face. After a few minutes of exchanged tears, the young woman dragged her father by the hand toward them.

"Papa, I'd like you to meet my friend, Isabelle. She helped me through this."

Allard bowed to Isabelle, who executed an awkward curtsey. "Thank you for helping my daughter. I will be forever in your debt."

Isabelle flushed, staring at the floor. "That's not necessary, I'm sure."

Allard put his arm around his daughter's shoulders and squeezed.

"I think we should handsomely reward this young woman, don't you?"

Annette beamed, staring up at her father. "Absolutely, Papa!"

Isabelle shook her head, hugging Thomas. "I have all I need here." She smiled at Marcus and Simon. "These are the people I love and trust, and they'll take me back to my family." She stared down the hallway at the dozens who had been rescued. "If you want to repay me, make sure all of the others get home to their families, no matter how difficult."

Allard bowed deeply. "You have my word."

Durant Residence

Paris, Kingdom of France

"What happens now?"

Sir Denys frowned at Marcus, and the Templar knew he wasn't going to like the answer. "I'm afraid not much will be done, if anything."

Simon stared at him, shocked. "Why not?"

"You wouldn't believe who we caught in there. Members of the court, foreign dignitaries, members of the clergy." Denys sighed. "It's really disheartening. I always felt this city was drenched with sin, but never did I think it infested the upper echelons of society."

Marcus' jaw clenched at the mention of the clergy taking part in the disgusting orgy of depravity that had been happening behind the walls of what was known as Babylon. "Surely something can be done. Something *must* be done."

Denys shook his head. "I'm sorry. Even Lord Allard wasn't able to convince them. We were forced to let everyone go that had been detained. They're simply too powerful, and it would prove too embarrassing to prosecute." He threw up his hands. "An order came in from the Court only minutes after you left, stating they were taking over the investigation, and by order of the King, there would be no public mention of what had been discovered."

Simon growled. "So that, of course, means nothing will be done, nobody will be brought to justice, and these heathens will be free to do it again."

"I'm afraid so, though they'll need to do it elsewhere."

Marcus' eyes narrowed. "What do you mean?"

"Lord Allard was so irate with the news, he and his men torched the estate."

Simon smiled. "Then at least one good thing came of this."

Denys nodded. "Yes, and we of course saved all those girls, including the lovely Isabelle." Denys bowed slightly in her direction as Marcus acknowledged the smiling girl, Thomas with his arms around her, her head buried in his chest.

Marcus' pleasure at the sight of her was short lived. "Yes, but what about the next girl? And the one after that? If we don't stop these people, it will never end."

Denys sighed. "This has been happening since the beginning of time, and will continue to happen until the end of time. As long as there are people who have desires that can't be met, there will be a need for establishments like Babylon. We have to be content in the knowledge that we saved scores of future women from sexual slavery, and freed those already trapped. Young Isabelle is safe, as is Lord Allard's daughter, and so many more. The young women are being returned to their homes, and the nuns are taking in those who won't communicate. Hopefully, in time, they'll be able to speak and tell us where they are from, though I fear some have gone mad with the thoughts of what happened to them."

Isabelle shuddered. "It terrifies me to imagine what they were going to do to me."

Thomas held her closer. "At least that imposter priest has been stopped. He can't go around doing this anymore."

Simon grunted. "Are we sure? They took him too. Who knows what will happen to him. And what about the man behind this? Surely someone was in charge."

Isabelle raised a finger. "Umm, there was. Or at least, I think there was."

Everyone turned their attention to her, causing her cheeks to flush. "Go on," prompted Marcus with an encouraging smile.

"Well, I met someone when we arrived earlier today. I think he was in charge, and if not, he seemed important at least."

"Who?" asked Denys, stepping closer, eagerness in his tone.

She shrugged. "I don't know. He never said his name."

Denys frowned. "That's unfortunate."

"I think he might have been some sort of priest."

Eyes shot wide around the room. Marcus leaned forward. "What makes you think that?"

"Well, he had a large gold cross around his neck, and he wore long red robes that sort of looked like what a priest might wear." She shrugged. "I've only ever seen our priest and a few others that visited, and none of them ever wore anything as fine as this man did, so I'm really not sure."

Marcus suppressed a curse, but Denys didn't bother. He stared at the nobleman. "It can't be, can it?"

Denys shook his head vehemently. "But it has to be! There's only one cardinal in Paris, and he's the only clergyman who can wear robes of that color."

Simon seethed. "A cardinal in charge of such depravity? It's unthinkable!"

Marcus sat, his faith shaken. "But it makes perfect sense. He tried to stop us from looking into this, even threatening us and the Order, Mercier said he met with the Cardinal and told him about his belief that all beautiful women were possessed, and that he wanted to save them. And it was only after this that the monks showed up with the so-called Lost Cause, begging for help, and then offering to assist him in his desire to perform exorcisms on beautiful women."

Denys' head bobbed in agreement. "Yes, so perhaps the Cardinal recognized an opportunity to use him to gather beautiful women from outside Paris, where they were less likely to encounter resistance, then bring them back to his den of horrors."

Marcus jabbed the air with his forefinger. "Exactly! With Mercier obsessed, he'd have a steady supply of new women coming in to satisfy his clientele. Their scared families would willingly hand them over, then when they didn't return, it would just be assumed they had died during the exorcism."

Isabelle was horrified, her eyes wide, her cheeks pale. "But why would he do this? Why would he be involved with such a place?"

Thomas shrugged. "Money?"

Denys shook his head. "Leverage."

Marcus' eyes narrowed. "What?"

Denys took a seat, his eyes staring at the fire as he assembled his thoughts. "He would know every single person that came and went, and what their perversions were. He could then use that information to force the leaders of our kingdom to do his bidding."

Simon spat. "Sickening! Disgusting!"

Marcus frowned. "Yet all too plausible." He sighed heavily. "And there's absolutely nothing we can do about it."

Simon clenched a fist. "And why not? We have proof!" He pointed at Isabelle. "She saw him. And so did the others!"

Marcus gently shook his head. "And would you put their lives at risk?" He gestured at Isabelle. "Would you put her life at risk?" Marcus rose, pacing in front of the fire for a moment. "And then there's the fact that any who could do something about it are probably being blackmailed by the Cardinal." He stopped, facing the group. "No, we must get Isabelle home, now, and put this entire incident behind us, otherwise we risk her life and that of the others." He stared at a cross mounted over the door. "I fear, however, that we have made an enemy today, one that could put us, and the Order, at risk."

Leblanc Residence

Crécy-la-Chapelle, Kingdom of France

"Mama, Papa!"

Isabelle leaped from her horse and raced toward her parents, her father chopping wood, her mother filling a jug with water. Her father dropped his axe, her mother the water, and both rushed toward her, their arms outstretched.

And Thomas' chest ached at the sight.

This was a family, unlike any he could really remember. His mother had died years ago, his father just last year, and a moment like this would never be in his future, unless one day it was his child throwing herself into his arms like Isabelle was now.

He wanted that.

Desperately.

He needed to be part of something, and that something had to be something pure, not the group of fiends he now worked with. The fact they now treated him with concern, as if he were a friend, had him terrified.

But Isabelle could save him.

If they married, she could come live with him in the city, and she would be his anchor to sanity while he toiled his days away for Mrs. Thibault and her henchman Enzo. He would make good money doing their bidding, then come home to his loving family and forget his troubles.

It had worked for his father for decades.

He had been a forger, for years creating documents indistinguishable from the real thing, and he had done it from the ground floor of their home. His mother had never minded, and they had always had a reasonable life, though it was always difficult.

At least with his current status, his work was nowhere near his home, where his family would reside, and he was making far better money than his father could have ever imagined.

A pit formed in his stomach as he watched the tearful reunion continue.

His father's work had gotten him killed, and had nearly cost Thomas his life.

Would you want that for your family?

His shoulders slumped and his face slackened as he realized the truth. The work he did could prove dangerous to the woman he loved, and any family they might bring into the world. Paris was a depraved city. Perhaps no more than any other, but it was the only one he knew. He could never ask Isabelle to marry him, to move to Paris, while he worked for Thibault.

You could move here.

He stared at the farm. It was humble. Simple. It gave every indication of a hard life.

But it was a life.

A good life.

A pure life.

Yet it would mean leaving behind everything he knew.

Though wasn't that what he was asking of Isabelle? How was it any fairer of him to ask her to move to Paris, giving up everything she knew, than it was for her to expect him to come here, doing the same. And at least here she had family. In Paris, all he had were memories.

It was an impossible choice.

And the fact that it was, told him he wasn't ready to make the commitment necessary to have the family that he now watched as they cried and hugged and bombarded each other with questions, the answers interrupted by the next query.

"Thomas! Come!"

Thomas forced a smile and walked over to join the family. Isabelle wrapped an arm around him, her face stained with tears of joy, and a smile that warmed his doubting heart.

"Thomas saved me."

He flushed. "I-I can hardly take credit. I was more along for the ride than anything else."

Isabelle patted his chest. "Nonsense! He challenged his employer into releasing a young woman held against her will, he rode into battle to help save Sir Marcus and Simon when they were outnumbered twenty to one, and he helped storm the estate where I and the others were held. He was magnificent!"

Thomas was left slack-jawed, wondering whether she was lying to impress her parents with his deeds so that they perhaps might like him more than he knew they did, or whether she had rewritten the version of events as she had been told into something that made her think more of him than he deserved.

Either way left him slightly disappointed, and definitely uncomfortable.

Then her parents embraced him, thanking him profusely, and he was now committed. He caught Isabelle's eye as she stood back, letting the display of affection for him continue, and she winked.

"You're terrible!" he mouthed, and she grinned.

And he let himself enjoy the moment, no matter how exaggerated the reasons for it were.

Isabelle's father grabbed him by the hand. "Come inside and warm yourself, son."

Thomas' chest ached and he didn't dare speak. He blinked back the burn that threatened to overwhelm his eyes at the sound of that one word, that one word that told him he had found his new family.

Son.

De Rancourt Residence

Crécy-la-Chapelle, Kingdom of France

Tanya bounded ahead, Marcus' nephew Jacques spotting them first. His cries of delight attracted the other children and denizens of the household, and within moments they were surrounded. It had been a longer than normal journey, two days instead of one, with Jeremy relegated to a cart that demanded a slow pace lest his ribs be jostled.

They had sent Isabelle and Thomas ahead yesterday so that her reunion wouldn't be delayed with her family, and he had made certain they had arrived safely a few minutes ago.

As he dismounted, he exchanged hugs with the children and bows with Lady Joanne and Beatrice, quickly followed by uncomfortable—for him—hugs from both. They tried the same with Simon but he partially drew his sword.

David accepted them with delight, and Jeremy with painful yelps once helped out of the cart.

"What happened to you?" asked Lady Joanne. "You rushed out of here and we didn't see you again."

"I was being a hero, of course."

She frowned. "Apparently you need more practice."

David howled with laughter. "Apparently you need more practice! It's so true!"

Jeremy scowled at him as he limped toward the barracks at the top of the hill. "If my ribs weren't broken, I'd give you a lashing."

Joanne's eyes narrowed. "Your ribs are broken?"

"Yes."

"Then you'll be staying in the house with us. You need plenty of rest and tending to, and a warm, soft bed. Not those inhumane conditions up there."

He hesitated. "Umm, will there be bathing?"

Joanne stopped and stared at him, Beatrice's face dominated by a grin. "Do you want there to be bathing?"

Jeremy's jaw dropped. "Oh God, no!"

Beatrice took him by the arm. "Oh, I'll bathe you, little one. You'll be squeaky clean like the day you were born."

Jeremy stared over his shoulder at Marcus with a "help me" expression if there ever was one. The moment he was out of sight, they all roared with laughter.

"Hello!"

Marcus turned to see Thomas and Isabelle walking up the pathway, hand-in-hand. "Is something wrong?"

Isabelle gave him a look. "Does something need to be wrong for us to pay you a visit?"

Marcus frowned at having jumped to conclusions. Joanne batted his arm before he had a chance to apologize.

"Of course not, dears, of course not."

"Isabelle!"

Marcus turned to see young Garnier rushing down the hill then trip and tumble several times before somehow springing to his feet without losing a beat. It was an impressive display of awkward recovery. He skidded to a halt in front of them.

"Thank God you're alive!" He clasped his hands against his chest. "I'm so sorry for what I did. I was, well, jealous, angry, hurt. I don't know what I was thinking. I know none of it is an excuse, but—"

Thomas stepped forward. "Wait a minute, are you Garnier?"

"Yes."

Thomas belted the boy in the face, laying him out cold on the snow. "Damn," he cried, shaking his hand. "I was hoping he'd still be awake so I could yell at him."

Simon leaned over, looking at the knocked out opponent. "I could wake him for you."

David nodded. "How about I tie him to a chair for you, then you can give him a real going over?"

Joanne wagged a finger at him. "He deserved that, but that's it. He's been working this farm like nobody's business since you've all been gone. He's done his penance, and deserves a chance for a proper apology. From what you two told me yesterday, this wasn't really his fault. This fake priest is to blame, not some poor boy hurt because of things overheard that should have never been said."

Thomas' chin dropped into his chest. "I'm sorry."

Joanne patted him on the cheek. "No need to be sorry. Like I said, he deserved the punch." She jerked a thumb at Simon and David. "It's what these two barbarians wanted to do that was crossing the line."

Simon frowned in mock shame. "We *do* tend to do that."

David agreed. "From time to time."

"But we mean well."

"Always."

"And it won't happen again."

"It probably will."

Joanne spun at them. "Would you two shut up?"

Two grins greeted her.

And she burst out laughing. "Oh, how I've missed you all." She headed for the door. "Come, let's get inside, and you can tell me all about your adventures, and what happened to those responsible. Surely Isabelle was mistaken when she said nobody had been punished."

Marcus let the rest enter the house, then stared at Garnier, still out cold on the snow. He frowned at the sight.

"I'm afraid you're the only one who ever saw any justice in this matter, my boy."

Notre-Dame de Paris Cathedral

Paris, Kingdom of France

Father Mercier sat in a rather plain room. There was a desk with a chair behind it, and the chair he was now sitting in. Other than that, there were two sconces holding torches, a lone candle on the desk, and a window to the outside showing him the only daylight he had seen in days.

And nothing else.

He wasn't sure where he was, except that it was Paris. He had been blindfolded then taken from the prison he was in, loaded into a carriage, then brought somewhere, not far, then walked, still blindfolded, to his current location. The blindfold had been removed, he was told to sit, then nothing.

That was at least half an hour ago, he was sure.

"What do you think is going on?"

His Lord Jesus Christ, standing near the window, shook his head. "You'll know shortly, my son."

"Is it bad?"

Jesus smiled gently. "It will be nothing more than you can handle, I promise."

Mercier sighed, content at his savior's words. "Then I will trust in you, as always." So far, his constant companion had remained just that, never leaving his side in these trying times, and as long as He was with him, everything would be fine. "Tell me of my mother. Is she well?"

"She is with us."

Mercier leaped from his chair, searching the room. "Where?"

"She is beside me, but you cannot see her. She is happy, and she is free from the burden placed on her so long ago by the forces of darkness."

Mercier dropped back into his chair, tears flowing down his cheeks. "Mama, can you see me?"

"She can."

"T-tell her I love her, and that I miss her."

"She can hear you."

He closed his eyes, trying to picture her from all those years ago, but all he could see was the writhing creature held to the table by his father and the priest as they failed to save her.

Yet *he* had.

"Are you proud of me, Mama?"

"She is."

The door swung open and he leaped to his feet, hurriedly wiping his eyes dry as Cardinal Nicolas entered the room. "Y-Your Eminence,

I wasn't expecting to see you again."

Nicolas eyed him for a moment. "You've been crying?"

"Yes, I'm sorry. For my mother. She's been released from her own personal Hell, and now stands with our Lord Jesus Christ in Heaven."

Nicolas sat behind the desk. "Yes, of course she does. I'm happy to hear it." He motioned to the chair Mercier had been sitting in. "Please, sit. You've had quite the ordeal."

"Doing the Lord's work is not always easy."

"No, it isn't, though you've done an excellent job of it, as I understand."

Mercier smiled and bowed his head. "Thank you, Your Eminence. I didn't think you approved."

Nicolas leaned back in his chair. "I didn't, but I was mistaken." He regarded Mercier for a moment. "Have you ever been mistaken?"

Mercier's eyes widened. "Of course, Your Eminence! Only God is infallible."

"Exactly. And I think it is a spiritual thing to admit when one is wrong, and to embrace what one once rejected, don't you?"

"Absolutely."

Nicolas folded his arms. "Word has reached me of the fine work you've been doing, and the troubles you've recently experienced."

Mercier sighed. "Yes, it was most unfortunate. Those Templars interfered with God's work."

Nicolas nodded. "Yes, they did, and they will be punished for it, if not by me, then by the Lord Himself."

"He speaks the truth."

Mercier smiled at the Lord, still near the window, still only revealing

His presence to himself. "I too believe that justice will be served."

Nicolas knocked hard on the desk three times. The door opened again and a dozen robed monks entered, lining up in a semi-circle on the far wall, their heads bowed. Nicolas rose and Mercier jumped to his feet. "Are you ready to go back to work?"

Mercier smiled, a rapturous joy spreading through him as his Lord walked over to him and placed a hand on his shoulder. "I am."

"And it will be glorious."

THE END

ACKNOWLEDGMENTS

The idea for this novel came from a line in the previous book where Jeremy says to his friend David, "I hear there's a witch in the woods. Maybe I'll seek her out in the morning and make sure she puts a curse on you." This line immediately had me thinking of witches, and all things related, and before I had finished the last book, I already had the kernel of an idea for this one. I settled on an exorcist, rather than a witch, for obvious reasons once I had determined the plot.

As to the plot itself, it was inspired by the modern day sex trade, an unbelievably robust business that goes far beyond the darkest reaches of our imagination. As I stated in a previous book, in the United States alone, in 2017, over 300,000 women and girls went or were missing. The number is staggering to the point of being unbelievable, yet it is true.

While many of the cases were solved, of those that weren't, some are probably safe and in hiding, living another life for whatever reason, but too many have been sold into an industry that is as old as time itself.

As usual, there are people to thank. My dad, as always, for the research, Deborah Wilson for some equine info, my Facebook followers including Seth Weintraub, Carol Hartley, Marc Quesnel, Jan Ronk, Jon Fraser, Lindy Jones Zywot, Meadowlin Kyress, and Steve Stranz for sharing their experience with breaking their ribs, and Susan "Miss Boss" Turnbull for some grammar help. And, of course, my wife, daughter, mother, and friends, for their continued support, and a special thanks to the proofreading and launch teams!

To those who have not already done so, please visit my website at www.jrobertkennedy.com, then sign up for the Insider's Club to be notified of new book releases. Your email address will never be shared or sold.

Thank you once again for reading.

Made in the USA
Las Vegas, NV
13 February 2021